The Deleted Heir

THE CONNECTED SERIES

THERESA PAPA

D0879685

AMPAPA L.L.C.

THE DELETED HEIR

ISBN- 978-1-7333091-9-6 (Ebook)

ISBN- 978-17333091-8-9 (Paperback)

Library of Congress Control Number: 2021915732

❀ Created with Vellum

One

MARCO FIORI

Present-day. Twenty-eight years old.

It's like carrying around a jagged heavy stone in your pocket. Some days you forget it's there. Other days you put your hand in your pocket and the smooth edge just makes you remember. Then on the worst days, you put your hand in and get scraped by the jagged edge bringing back all the pain and sadness in your soul.

"Marco, look at me!" She waves her hands in front of my face. "It's over!"

I'm relieved more than anything. My mind was wandering while she nagged on and on. Caitlin is beautiful I'll give her that. But I've been just going through the motions with her for a while. She wants a commitment of which I'm not capable.

"Leave," she barks. "Leave!" Cate throws open the door.

"I'm sorry Cate," I whisper putting my head down. God knows I'm the asshole whose attention span is lacking. This is always how it happens, my mind somewhere in the past grieving. My lack of responsiveness always the final straw that brings every relationship to an explosive end. Being by myself is easier, leaves more time for work. Maybe it's better if I'm alone.

Two

AMELIA DRAGONETTI (MIMI)

PRESENT-DAY. Twenty-one years old.

"You'll know soon enough what it's like to have a *Fiori fantasy!*" The tall blond laughs, as she hands me a card. A few minutes earlier, she introduced herself as Kimber. I type the address from the card into my phone's GPS. Kimber gestures for me to take a seat.

"How much could he have changed since I knew him five years ago?" I shrug. "He's been best friends with my older brother since kindergarten. Sure, he has nice features, but he was tall and lanky."

She slowly shakes her head and presses her shiny lips together.

"No?" I cock my head to the side. "To be honest, I always thought he was nerdy and overprotective. When I was a child, Marco would be at our house every single day. He and my brother Tony were inseparable. They'd always make fun of me together."

"Tell me more." She leans forward, resting her chin on her fist.

"As soon as my brother's guitar teacher arrived on Tuesdays and Thursdays, Marco would always play with me. It lasted until they were teenagers, and I was almost seven." I grin to myself, reminiscing.

"See, he's really sweet," Kimber says, gushing. "I just knew under all that broody brawn lies a heart of gold."

I wave my index finger. "Then, suddenly, it was as if they were both too cool to acknowledge me. He was abruptly quiet and kept to himself mostly. The two of them went out instead of hanging around the house. A few years later, they both left for college."

"Hmm, maybe the age difference kicked in for a while." She places her index finger on her shiny bottom lip. "He's still a man of few words until you get to know him, though."

"Yeah, during breaks from the university, he would appear all of a sudden and then leave again. I guess you could say he was like a friendly older brother." I nod.

She walks around the desk and sits on the edge. "Yeah, like I said, he still has the quiet, brooding thing going on, and he's tall. But lanky and nerdy are the opposite of what he is now. That man is the star in all the girls' fantasies around here. He has thick wavy hair; incredibly broad shoulders, and his muscular arms seem to want to burst out of his t-shirts." She looks up at the ceiling imagining the man she describes. "The interior designer drools when she talks about him. She's angry that he's not using her on the Pope reconstruction. I guess the owner's wife, Samantha, is a designer or something." Kimber unwraps a piece of chewing gum and stuffs it into her mouth.

"I'm sure he'll still think of me like a younger sister since he's my older brother's age. And I'll probably feel like he's nagging me about my unwise life choices just like Tony does." I wave my hand in the air dismissively. "So, no fantasies here." *He never liked anyone I dated. He'll probably lecture me about my lack of direction in life and work.*

She pops a huge bubble. "Talk to me next week after your lucky ass works closely with him *alone* at the remodel." Her eyebrows go up and down with a giggle. "Even though he's way too old for me, I've had a few fantasies in my spank bank starring Marco."

If I had to guess Kimber's age, she looks about eighteen or nineteen. Three years younger than me, at least. I laugh at her comment and shake my head.

"So, will you be working in the office over at the mansion too?"

"We have a few more weeks to finish up here, and then I'll be trucking on over there." She winks.

"That's good! I think I would go crazy without someone to talk to all day." I shrug my shoulders, rise from the chair, and slip the card into my pocket. I need to go if I'm going to be on time. "Thanks for the update, it's nice to meet you, Kimber."

"Great to meet you too! Can't wait to have lunch together." She flips her long blond hair over to one side.

"Sure." I give a little wave and walk out.

Three

MARCO FIORI

I PULL up slowly at the place formerly known as Club Beta to admire the castle-like exterior. A jet-black steeply arched roof sets off four majestic stories of cut grey stone. The morning sun highlights the faceted, rippled texture. Two grand turrets surround a third-floor concave balcony in front. As I drive around the side, there is an identical set in the back. Under the front balcony, in an oversized arched entranceway, is where *she's* waiting. I pick up the pace and park in my spot to run over and open the door for her. Poor thing is shivering in the unpredictable October Chicago weather. Why is it, women insist on putting looks above warmth and functionality when picking out outfits?

"Sorry, I'm late. I'll get you a key, so this won't happen again." I hold the door open for her to enter.

"Thanks." She won't even look me in the eye. I can tell she's pissed at me like every woman I've encountered lately. All I can do is apologize and get her a key right away.

She silently slips through the door past me when I gesture with my arm. "Ladies first." I put all my stuff on the desk in the office while she looks around the small room.

Amelia Dragonetti is my assistant doing odd jobs, ordering, and logging in deliveries as we prepare for the transformation. She's five years older than the last time I saw her, it shows in her facial features, but she still has a small, petite frame. Her height can't be more than five foot two, and her shoe size still looks like a child's.

When she slips off her coat, I can really see her shape. The tiny circumference of her waist accentuates the curves of her hips and ass. When my eyes travel upward and skim over voluptuous tits, she clears her throat to call attention to what an asshole I am for checking her out. My neck snaps up eye to eye. *Not cool, Marco, behave yourself.*

"So little one, how have you been? How's the family?" This is awkward, so I ask questions to divert her attention. It fails.

She grins and makes no secret of checking me out as well. *Touché little one.* She hops up on the desk to sit. "Everyone is fine. We had some drama at the house in Lake Geneva last month, but it's all good now."

"Tony mentioned it was about Elizabeth and some game. Right?"

"Yeah, she's fine now, and my mom is past the trauma she went through." She plays with the lace trim of her shirt.

"What happened to Lucia?" I step closer, planting my palms on the oak desk.

"Elizabeth was being targeted by a creepy online game. Tony had her staying with us at the house in Lake Geneva. We had guards all over, and my dad had it locked up like Fort Knox, but the kidnappers still managed to get to Liz by threatening my mom." Her eyes meet mine.

"When I spoke to Tony last, he never mentioned the part about your mom. I need to visit them. I've been away much too long."

They became my family in the absence of my own in my childhood. My stomach drops thinking of how I've tried to stop depending on the Dragonettis'. It's been lonely. *I needed to stand on my own two feet.* "When bad things happen, it reminds us of the truly important things in life." I pat her shoulder with my hand. "Listen, Amelia, I want to apologize for making a scene the last time we saw each other at the grad party."

She shrugs her shoulders and tilts her head. "You were right all along. I was acting naïve and stupid. I stopped going out with Jimmy Bono as soon as the party was over."

"Deep down, I've always known how smart you are." I wink and give her a one-arm hug. As I pull her into my side, her scent engulfs my thoughts, vanilla, and cherries.

"So, what's my first assignment, boss? Fill me in." She swings her legs back and forth. I smile, remembering how cheerful and happy she always was and still is.

"We're the only two people in this historic building until construction starts. The crew will begin the rehab turning Club Beta, a fantasy nightclub," I indicate the surroundings with my hands outstretched. "into The Pope House, a home for children with nowhere to live. In addition, the whole top floor will be the personal residence of Nico Pope and his soon-to-be wife, Samantha."

Amelia interrupts. "I know Nico and Samantha! Remember? Their Tony's friends too."

I chuckle at her spirit, trying to prove how mature she's become. "Well, did you also know, she works as an attorney representing children? In some court cases, when their parents are defendants, the kids have nowhere to live. They can stay at Pope House during the long court process. Kind of like a huge foster home that's temporary."

She smirks, "I'll admit I didn't know that."

I touch my fingertip to the tip of her nose because I can't help myself. "See? I'm full of information. Just ask when you want to know something."

"How about telling me what to do, boss."

I regain my composure and fill my mind with work once again. "Let's organize this workspace and make a list of office supplies to order by the end of the day. I'll be in the dance hall making some calls about the pool."

"No problem. Which desk do you want?" Her head tilts with a dimpled smile.

"It makes no difference to me, you pick." I glance back from the doorway to see her hop down getting to work right away. For some reason, I can't stop smiling.

Mimi's always had a positive effect on me since I was little. My memories of us conjure up happiness in my soul.

Then: Age Ten

The fighting and hatred between my mom and dad have made me want to escape to the Dragonetti's again today. My best friend Tony's family have taken me in as one of their own since my sister's accident.

"Hey, Mama D! Where's Tony?"

"He's having his guitar lesson, Marco."

"Mawcooooo!" Tony's four-year-old little sister, Amelia, comes running into the kitchen and jumps up into my arms.

"Hi, Meems. Watcha doin today?" I always love playing with Mimi when I feel lonely or down. She lights up the world with her smile.

"You're my best fwend. Come pway wif me." She grabs my hand, dragging me into the family room. Mama D just chuckles and continues cooking dinner. Mimi sits me down in a shrunken chair next to a pint-size table.

"Sit here, Mawco. I gonna make you my gwoom. I da bwide." I laugh out loud when she puts what looks like a communion veil on her head and clips a bow tie on my shirt. She's the only one that has the power to make me laugh today.

After our whole fake wedding with plastic cake and teacups. She sits on my lap and hugs me with a kiss on my cheek. I hug her tight feeling better than I have in a long time.

"Looks like my sister has you wrapped around her little finger."

Tony is standing by the door laughing at us, but I don't care. Mimi is my happiness.

"Come on, let's go. The guys are waiting at the park for us."

I kiss Mimi on the head and say goodbye, following Tony out the door looking back at her little hand in the air.

"Hey, Tone, thanks for not making fun of me playing with a four-year-old."

"Listen, man, my sister means the world to me, and you make her smile. That's all that matters. Did you see her face last week at her birthday gift from you? I think it's great. Thank you."

Four

MIMI

The office needs a good cleaning before organizing our desks and ordering supplies. I decide to leave the desks facing each other to make it conducive for Marco and me to communicate without turning around. Then I begin unloading his boxes of files and personal stuff into his desk. He must love pictures because I'm unwrapping several framed photos when I come to one with my whole family in it. I was still a baby. My mom's standing over me while I sit on Marco's lap. My face is split in two with a big smile, looking up at him.

"That's my favorite picture of all of us." I'm startled at the sound of his deep voice behind me. "Your family is the best!" He leans in close enough for me to inhale his masculine scent without touching.

"I'm too little to remember this being taken. But we all look happy. Somehow, when we are little, we don't realize how great it is to not have a care in the world. We just play and pretend."

"That was the happiest time in my life. Your parents always treat me like one of their own. It was at a time when I needed it." He turns and sits, "Someday I'll tell you the story," then clears his throat.

"Should I display all the photographs on the shelving unit?" I start wiping them down.

"Great idea, I think we'll be very comfortable here." He studies the pictures on his desk.

"Me too."

I begin arranging books and photos creatively on the shelves while Marco makes a few calls. He looks casual with his legs spread wide and his head tilted back, looking at the ceiling. I take my chances to study him while he's not paying attention. A sexy neck, corded with muscle, and his Adam's apple completes the masculine vignette. I look away for a minute so that my perusal of his features isn't noticeable.

After an acceptable amount of time passes from this new angle, I go back to my examination. From this angle, his sharp jawline and smooth skin lead up to lips with just the right cushion. I pick up a stack of folders and walk them to his credenza behind him. All I can see beyond his thick brown hair is the copious number of dark lashes that flutter when he blinks. I recall when I was a little girl, thinking his eyes were kind and trustworthy. No wonder when caramel-colored pupils are enhanced so beautifully.

A file box is marked for the basement, and I motion to him that I'm going downstairs. He smiles, nods, and continues his call.

The mansion is huge and still filled with all the props from Club Beta. The three-story room I have to walk through to get to the wide stone staircase at the far end is eerily quiet. It served as the main dance area. The dancefloor is easily the size of a football field. Glass enclosures still hang from the ceiling where dancers performed. Large inflatable pools are now empty rectangles leaning against the wall. The marble and stone railings on the balconies above add to the chill in the rectangle room.

The stone staircase becomes wider at the bottom as I step down into the lower level. I should have brought a flashlight noticing the red candle wax in the niches along the corridor. The cold stone under my fingertips as I feel for the light switch sends a quiver through me. The lever turns on medieval-style sconces that don't help much with illumination. The storeroom's pine door is unlike all the others in the hallway. They are heavy dark wood, with crosshatch steel bars, over a hinged peephole. I place the file box on the dusty desk in the storeroom and hear rustling out in the hallway. When I investigate, there's no one there but a cord from audiovisual equipment in the middle of the cement floor. I pick it up and wonder if Marco is down here with me.

"Marco? Hello? Are you down here?" *Crickets. The hairs on the back of my neck stand at attention.*

A little creeped out, I ascend the stairs, ears still peeled for any sounds, but nothing, just the click of my shoes against the stones. Marco looks up when I plop the cord in front of him.

"What's this for?" He asks.

"Didn't you drop it when you were in the basement?" I shrug.

"I haven't been in the basement today." He turns the cord over in his hand.

"Really?" I sit on his desk beside him and cross my legs. His eyes roam my body, and it sets off an inferno under my skirt. When his eyes meet mine, I continue. "I heard someone down there with me. Are there men here working today?"

He pushes backward in his rolling desk chair and stands.

"None of the workers will start until my last job is finished up. Maybe I should check it out down there. I'll be right back."

Five

MARCO

I RUN down the stairs to the lower level, relieved to put some space between myself and Amelia. After all these years, my genuine caring for her has turned into something more. I can't let this attraction evolve if we will be alone here for weeks. Tony will have my head on a stick if I make a move on her. There are seven years between us. Someone like her deserves a man who can love her deeply without worry or depression. It's going to take every drop of willpower I have in me to get through this.

When I come to the end of the corridor, I can hear the wind coming into the building from somewhere. The door leading out to the lower-level garage is partially open, the chill from the temperature outside permeates my cotton shirt. My foreman Jason must have overlooked locking it when he was here yesterday. I close it tight, lock it, then head back up the stairs. When I walk into the office, she's already back at work. I opt to goof around with her to make things between us more like friends cause the attraction is thick and needs to be unheeded.

"Hey, can we talk?" I lean against my desk.

She picks her head up, and her warm honey color eyes meet mine. "What's up?"

"I didn't want to frighten you earlier, but this old building was constructed in 1892, and there have been stories that it may be haunted. The sound you witnessed could be a manifestation of the supernatural variety." It's difficult to keep a straight face.

She snorts, rising from her chair. "Seriously, you believe in that stuff?" Her eyebrows scrunch together as she plays with the ancient paperweight on her desk.

"I'm just saying it may be an explanation for the unexplainable." I shrug, retreating behind my desk to sit. When I look up, she has a shocked look on her face and tears in her eyes. "Oh my God, little one, I was joking, I promise." In a blink, I'm across the room, holding her in my arms to console her. She wraps her arms around my torso, hugging me back. "It was just the door by the garage that sticks. My foreman must have forgotten to check it. Don't be afraid. I'm so sorry." I quickly get the words out to calm her. The strength she puts into her hug and the scent of her shampoo makes me warm all over.

"It's okay." She wipes her tears with the back of her hand. I grab a tissue from the moving box on the desk and hand it to her. She accepts it with a watery grin. "The reason I'm kind of freaked out is that last year after papa died, I saw him in his bedroom one morning. My grandmother thinks I'm in tune with the spirit world."

"You actually saw your grandfather? Did he speak to you?" I'm still holding both of her little hands in mine.

She shakes her head before replying. "No, he smiled at me. I wasn't afraid of him because ... you know... he's my papa. But if I saw any other ... um ... you know... I would freak out."

"And you're sure it wasn't a dream?"

She nods. "I was wide awake."

I bend a little to come to eye level with her. "Just remember I'm here for you no matter how busy I am you, come first. If you're frightened or even just creeped out, call me from your cellphone. Or scream my name, and I'll come running."

Turning, she lets go. "Thanks." She sits down in her chair and pulls her hair back into a ponytail with the black elastic band on her wrist.

"What do you feel like eating for lunch? Let's get out of here and go eat." I close the books on my desk.

"Are you sure? It's a little early." Her head tilts to the side.

"That's why I'm the boss, so I can go to lunch when I feel like it. And stay as long as I want." I grab her coat and hold it up for her to put on. She stands and turns to put an arm on each side. "You should get a warmer coat."

"I have a warmer coat! Dad!" She rolls her eyes at me. "It's gonna be warmer this afternoon, and I hate being hot."

The weather has warmed up into the seventies from the chilly morning we had, so I opt to take Amelia to the Waterfront Café near Sheridan and Rosemont. The parking spot is on a side street, and we both are surprised to see Samantha and Nico coming out of the building there.

"Hey, you guys! How's the wedding planning coming?"

Samantha hands Nico her bag and hugs Amelia and me. "It's all good we've been busy."

"Well, don't worry about the house, Amelia and I started getting things ready today. We're getting in an early lunch at The Waterfront. You want to join us?"

"Sorry, we can't today, I have a dress fitting, and Nico has a client in an hour. We will definitely go soon, though, and discuss the pool in the main dance hall."

"I want to see if it's possible to have a retractable dance floor over the pool," Nico says. "Remember, in the movie *It's A Wonderful Life*?" He smiles.

"Wow, that's a great idea!" Amelia chimes in.

"Okay, let me know, I'm ready whenever you have time. I'll research that new idea of yours, buddy. See ya later." They get into Nico's Tesla and drive off.

There won't be many more days to enjoy outdoor dining this year. The restaurant is rustic and eclectic in the food choices. I order the lobster roll, and Amelia gets the chicken salad inside an avocado with a milkshake for dessert. The line at the counter goes fast, and we take our food to a table. Overhead are strings of outdoor patio lights zigzagging from one end of the lakeside deck to the other. Water laps gently against the rocks in a lulling reiteration.

We sit facing the water, just the corner of the table between us instead of across. The breeze blows back her silky brown hair. She looked beautiful when it was up off her face in a ponytail. But as soon as we pulled up to the restaurant, she unleashed it over her shoulders again. When it wafts across her forehead, I think I might have to sit on my hands to keep from brushing the strand away.

"Thank you for this. I know you're just trying to make me feel better after this morning." She places her fork next to her plate and grins.

"I should know better than to tease you like that. Even when you were a child, you believed every story. I fabricated quite a few to entertain you while Tony took his guitar lessons."

"Are you saying I'm as gullible as I was when I was seven?" She throws a cherry tomato at me.

"Don't even start with the food fight, little one. You know I always win." I wink.

Her dimple appears when she smirks at my challenge. "I'm older and taller to be more of an opponent now, though." She straightens in her chair.

I wrap up the crumbs of my sandwich and get up to grab her plate to take to the garbage. She pulls it away and rises to bring her own. "Okay, be that way." I swipe my finger into the mountain of whipped cream on her shake and pop it on the tip of her nose. Her eyes get big, and she buries her lips between her teeth. I've never seen anything more adorable.

She takes the napkin and wipes her nose while I turn and head for the exit. She catches up with me on the sidewalk near my truck. "You're so lucky that I need this job and don't want to piss off my new boss because I would use this straw to flick some ice cream on you right now."

"See, I told you being the boss has privileges." She tries to shoulder-check me but forgets that her shoulder is a foot shorter than mine. I crack up.

Six

MIMI

"An indoor pool with a retractable dance floor over it. Is that possible?" I spin around on the wooden dance floor and look at Marco, waiting for an answer. I'm positive he noticed my skirt twirling with me, and I like the attention.

"It will be a feat in engineering but not impossible." He rubs the shadow forming on his chin. "I'll finally get to use my degree in engineering for an interesting project. I'm excited."

"What should I work on this afternoon, boss?"

"Are the supplies ordered already?"

"I have them all in my cart online but need the credit card for the order."

"Good, I have to add some drafting supplies. Here's a list." He reaches in his pocket and hands me the list and his credit card. "Make the delivery for tomorrow even if it's extra."

"You got it!" I wink at him like an idiot. *How embarrassing. What's wrong with me?*

In the afternoon, I help Marco load the blowup swimming pools into the back of a rental truck. We bring them to a women's shelter for their backyard next summer. After being bullied or abused by someone or finding themselves pregnant with no help. It empowers me to see these women making it on their own. They rise-up and do what's best for themselves and their kids. All the kids will love cooling off in the water on the humid, hot days in July.

After we unload, we head back to the mansion to get my car and end my first day. The traffic is heavy, and I let my mind wander to when I was seven years old and being *sort of* bullied in school.

Fifteen years earlier...

"Mimi, why did you hit Jimmy?" Mommy asked while she drove me home from school. I was sent to the principal's office and then home after slapping stupid Jimmy across the face.

"He won't stop buggin me!" I couldn't tell the principal or my mom that he kept pushing me behind the cubbies in the art room to kiss me. Today, Jimmy slobbered all over my face before I got away by slapping him hard.

"Next time, tell the teacher, and she can take care of the problem."

"Okay, mom." I rolled my eyes and looked out the window. The stupid idiot is so sneaky he made sure the teacher was occupied when he pounced on me.

A few hours later, Tony and Marco came home from school. I finished my homework and sat in the family room playing video games. Tony went to get ready for his guitar lesson, and Marco came to hang out with me.

"Hey, Meems. Can I play?"

I handed him the other controller. We played silently for a while.

"So, feel like telling me what happened today?"

"No." I vehemently shake my head.

"Come on, Meems. You know you can tell me anything, and I will always keep it a secret." He mimicked zipping up his lips and throwing away the key.

I giggled. Somehow, Marco always charmed me to do whatever he wanted. Marco was almost fourteen, and he knew all about boys and girls. *Maybe he would have good advice on how to get Jimmy to leave me alone.*

"You promise, you won't tell anyone."

He nodded his head with his lips zipped.

"Okay." I take a deep breath. "There's this boy Jimmy that wants to kiss me." His eyes got big, but he just nodded for me to go on. "He keeps pushing me behind the cubbies in the art room and forcing his mouth on me. I couldn't get him off me today, so I finally slapped him."

"You did the right thing, Meems. No one has the right to touch you without your permission."

"But my mom said I should have just told the teacher." I shrugged.

He licked his lips and raised his eyebrows. "Okay, I guess Mama's right. There should be an order to things. How about the next time he tries to kiss you tell the teacher? See what happens. If he tries another time and you can't get away, defend yourself so you can get away and tell the adults exactly what he's doing."

"Exactly?" He nodded. "But that's embarrassing." I didn't tell him the kid pulled my ponytail to keep my head still.

"I know it might be, but if you don't stand up for yourself now, it might get worse later."

"I'm not sure if I can be so brave. It's been hard telling you." I looked down at the carpet in thought.

"If worse comes to worst, I'll have a talk with Jimmy myself." His face scrunched up.

"You would do that?" Marco always cares enough to make my heart stop hurting.

Just like always, he hugged me to his chest, nodded his head, placed a kiss on top of mine.

Present-day…

I could use one of his hugs now. I smile, thinking, what a great hugger he's always been. That larger-than-life physique, looming over me with long muscular arms around me.

We're back at the mansion when Marco brings me out of my reverie.

"Thanks for all your help today, little one." He switches off the ignition and turns toward me. His big beautiful hands have long slender fingers still on the steering wheel. The transformation in his appearance since college makes me think of him differently. Not like a brother as I used to.

"See you tomorrow at 9 a.m. sharp." I wink. *I must stop doing that!*

"I'll have your own key for you tomorrow, I promise." He holds up his right hand.

"Are you gonna skip out on unloading the office supplies?" I chuckle and hop out.

"No, I can help you. I'm a hands-on boss." He grimaces at his possible double meaning. I bust out laughing and close the car door without a verbal response.

The fall leaves have collected on our front porch. Mom is outside sweeping them in a pile. I can smell leaves burning somewhere in the neighborhood as I lock my doors and walk up the path.

"Hi, mom!" I grab the shovel and hold it steady for her to sweep the leaves into it.

"Hello sweetie, how was your first day of work?"

"It was good. Marco took me to the Waterfront café for lunch."

She smiles, "That was nice of him. He's always taken good care of you. I never had to worry about your safety as a child when Marco was around." She empties the shovel into a garbage can.

The porch has a waist-high brick railing with a smooth cement cap surrounding the perimeter. I climb up on the cement cap to sit over in the corner so I could turn sideways, put my legs up on the ledge, and lean my back against the house. I cross my legs at the ankle against the cold cement.

"Why do you think that is, mom? Why would he care so much about his best friends' little sister who spied on them all the time?" I pick a wayward leaf off my coat.

My mom leans the broom against the railing and pulls the chair over closer to me to sit. "From the first day I brought you home from the hospital, he was taken with you. Marco would ask to hold you all the time. He spoke softly to you while he did and would kiss you on the head. And when you got older, your eyes would light up as soon as he entered the house."

"Weren't you ever worried about a seven-year-old boy paying me so much attention?"

"Your father and I discussed it, and we both were convinced that he acted that way because of his sister." Mom wrings her hands, looking down at them.

"Marco doesn't have a sister."

She looks back up at me with watery eyes. "She drowned in the family pool six months before you were born. Marco was devastated, and we welcomed him into our family any time he wanted to be with us."

"Oh, mom!" I jump down. "Why was I never told? That's so terrible."

"By the time you were old enough to understand, we had become Marco's sanctuary from the anguish and heartache going on in his own family. We never spoke about the drowning after Marco asked us not to. We wanted to respect his wishes, especially when he lost his mother shortly after. She couldn't cope with the loss.

"What happened? Why wasn't his sister being watched over?"

"They had a nanny watching her while the parents worked and Marco was in school. The sitter was on the phone, and the toddler crawled out the doggie door into the backyard. By the time she found the little girl, it was too late."

I feel sick to my stomach and go into the house. My face is wet, and I wipe the tears with my fingers as I run up the stairs. I plop on my bed and hug the pillow. Mom knocks gently on the door.

"Sweetie? You alright? I knew that would upset you, which is another reason we never told you. You see, we have always known about the bond between you and Marco. It's plain to see how much you care for him as well. He's family."

"I just feel so stupid with all the worry I've had over what I'm going to do with my life. The decision to wait to go to design school and get a job instead. It's all minor compared to what Marco's family has been through."

My mother sighs and sits on the edge of the bed, "Marco's mother and I became friends before you were born when Tony started on the hockey team. She was a nice person who had difficulty dealing with her baby's death. The family was devastated after the accident. Soon after you were born, his mother passed away, his father worked long hours, leaving him alone most of the time. He spent his days here with us. When his father remarried, Marco backed away from him abruptly. Although he saw his maternal grandmother frequently, she was sickly. His grandfather even asked daddy if we could look after Marco. Of course, daddy and I were willing to help in any way we could. I have a feeling one day he'll confide in you the whole story."

"When horrible things happen, it puts perspective on every decision we make."

"That's a very mature realization, sweetie. I'm glad you can finally see that things will work out just fine for you. When you took my advice and got a job working with Marco in the field you love, you did the right thing." She pats my hand.

"I know I'll learn a lot just being involved in the day-to-day stuff. Experiencing first hand what the career would be like on a daily basis in my future."

"Everyone should work or do internships in the career they aspire to before they commit to classes in college or grad school. It saves money and the grief of having a degree in a field you don't enjoy. Half the battle of having a career is loving what you do every day."

"Thanks, mom, for understanding about my indecision. You and daddy have been so great and patient with me."

"I'll stop with my words of wisdom you've heard many times before. Just know your dad and I are proud of whatever you decide to pick as a career." She hugs me. "We love you."

I hug her tight. "Love you too."

Seven

MARCO FIORI

"THE DELIVERY TRUCK just pulled in behind me," Amelia shouts from the front door.

I quickly get up from my desk and run out to help her with the boxes.

"Don't prop the door open cause Clyde will get out. I'll carry in the boxes. Hold the door open when I get there."

"Who's Clyde?" Her eyebrows get that cute little scrunch.

"He's my dog." I pile the boxes on top of each other and balance them in my arms.

"Should I be afraid? I bet he's a huge vicious one." Mimi points her index finger at me and twirls it in a circle. "An extension of your macho ego?" She giggles.

I roll my eyes, and she opens the door to find my little Yorkshire Terrier sitting there patiently waiting for my return. His enormous ears on full alert.

"That is hilarious!" She bends at the waist, holding her stomach with laughter. "But he's so cute I can't laugh at him! I'm just gonna laugh at you." She picks him up and follows me into the office, where I drop the load on the conference table. When I turn around, he's smelling her face, and she's speaking baby talk to him. "Aren't you a sweet little pup with a bigger-than-life name? Yes, you are." She makes smooch sounds at him with her lips. "Look at these ears! Oh, you like it when I scratch behind them. Huh? Dat feels so gooooood."

"Are you gonna just play with him all day, or are we getting work done?"

"Don't be a party pooper." She kisses Clyde. "Your daddy's a party pooper. Yes, he is. He's just mad that I can tease him relentlessly about you."

I've never seen Clyde's stump of a tail wag so fast. "Okay, get all the jokes out of the way so we can get to work today." I cross my arms and lean against my desk.

She sits with him in her lap with a huge grin pointing directly toward me. "I just would never peg you for a Yorkie kind of guy. Big muscular construction guys usually have a German Sheppard or a Pitbull." She shrugs.

"Yeah, Yeah, I get it all the time. The guys crack up whenever I bring him to poker night. I always get strange looks when I walk him too." I hide my smile under my hand as I rub my chin. "He was my grandmother's dog, and I couldn't let a stranger take him."

"I have to admit the little spiked collar adds something." She laughs through her nose. Scratching Clyde's neck under his collar.

"Nana moved into a retirement home last year, and the nurses there decided she's too frail to take proper care of him. I bring Clyde to see her when I visit, and it makes her happy." I shrug. "It's the least I could do." I push off the desk and sit in my chair, facing her.

"You're a softie under all that macho muscle and broody demeanor. I always knew it even when I was little, you have a heart of gold." I bite my bottom lip and shake my head at the fact, she has always known me inside and out.

"My grandmother named him Clyde after a jazz trumpet player Clyde McCoy from the early 1900s. I guess the guy actually has a star on the Hollywood Walk of Fame. The puppy was good company for Nana when she lived in the house alone after Papa's passing. She feels better knowing I have him."

She picks up Clyde to look into his little face, "And now you keep big macho Marco company... huh wittle won?" She giggles.

I walk around my desk to take Clyde, and I can't help but get a glimpse of Mimi's bra where my puppy crawled up her chest. She has amazing tits. I bend to put him in his bed at my feet. He rolls over, presents his tummy for a rubbing, and I oblige.

"I get the hint. I'll start unloading the boxes and put stuff away," she says.

Clyde sighs and snuggles into his bed for a nap while my mind wanders to ten years ago.

Then: Age 19

To be back in Mama D's kitchen eating my dish of pasta and meatballs is what I've been dreaming of since I left for college. The bowl in front of me makes my mouth water. Tony and I just got home for fall break. I came here first cause it's the place I think of as my home. The whole family is here at the table eating Sunday dinner with mama and papa D, as proud as could be. Daniel and Dominic fight over the last piece of garlic bread as mama D cuts more at the counter. Mimi twirls her pasta around her fork. She's turning into a beautiful young lady.

After dinner, I tell mama to go, sit while I do the dishes. Meems offers to help me. Even at twelve years old, she's still so petite except for her chest. It's hard not to notice with the rest of her still not caught up yet.

"How's college going?" She grins up at me.

"It's okay, sometimes, I miss your mom's cooking." I take the wet dish from her and load it into the dishwasher.

"How about you? How's school?"

She rolls her eyes and blows air through her lips. "I got suspended for three days."

I put down the dish I was washing and look her in the eye. "What happened?"

"Jimmy grabbed my boob, and I kicked him in the balls really hard." She shrugs. I put my hand in front of my mouth to cover my grin. She starts laughing too. "I'd had enough! And someone smart once told me that nobody has the right to touch me unless I give them permission."

"Oh yeah! You remember that, huh?" I nod in appreciation.

"Of course. I remember everything you tell me." She smiles up at me and sheds light on my world as she always has.

"So, do you think Jimmy got the message to keep his hands off you?" I consciously loosen my grip on a glass I'm holding so it won't crack and cut my hand.

"Who knows. That kid is relentless." She wipes down the counters with her back towards me. Thank goodness she can't see my rage.

"What's his last name?" I keep my voice steady.

"Bono."

"Is Louie Bono his older brother?" I slam the door closed on the dishwasher a little too hard.

"Yeah, why?" She turns.

"No reason. I went to school with that guy." I shrug, trying to calm myself. "Let's finish up cause Tony and I have plans tonight."

"You go ahead I'll finish." She throws her paper towel in the garbage.

"Thanks." I kiss her on the head like I always do on my way out the door.

Present-day

Amelia is quiet as we work, but she turned on some music on her phone. I can't seem to take my eyes off of her as she sashays to the tune while unpacking. She arranged our desks facing each other, and the image of her fills my peripheral vision. It's because her beauty lights up the whole room. Her golden skin tone and caramel-colored hair with huge eyes that are so expressive make me crazy. Her small delicate features, remind me of fairies and sprites in a movie I watched as a child. Then when I'm lucky enough to stand near her petite frame, I fantasize that she runs toward me, jumping up and wrapping her legs around my waist. Our faces are level, and our lips meet...

"Marco? Are you listening?"

Her sweet voice pulls me out of my wayward thoughts. I blink. "Sorry, what did you say?" My feet fall from perched on the desk, and I turn.

"I said that I was going to catalog all the paintings in the holding room. I'll be down the hall." She's standing in the doorway, hands on her hips.

"Yes, that's fine, thank you."

I watch as she leaves, checking her out from behind and loving every curve.

My cell rings its Amelia's brother Tony. He calls around this time every day to check on her.

"Hey, Tone, how's it goin?" I flip my pencil over my fingers back and forth.

"I'm fine, how's Mimi?" Amelia's friends and family all call her Mimi for a nickname, but I prefer to keep things more formal since I'm her boss now. *I only remember that half the time, though. I'm failing miserably in some areas.*

"She's doing well, very organized, and she's definitely not lazy."

"Good, I'm glad it's working out. Thanks again for the favor. I figured with you and Nico around to keep an eye on her, she is safe there."

"Got it covered."

"Good I'll see you next weekend my parents and I are going up to the house in Lake Geneva Tuesday and won't be back until then."

"See ya then, say hello to Liz."

"Will do."

After I hang up, I think about the last time I was in Lake Geneva and how I finally got to apologize to Mimi yesterday for my outburst.

Then: Age 23

College went by fast, and I'm graduating at the top of my engineering class. You would think Mama D gave birth to me she's so proud. The Dragonetti's are having a grad party at their Lake Geneva home for all our friends. I'm in the driveway helping unload the drinks from a van when Mimi pulls up with some of her friends. Her parents bought her a mustang convertible for her sixteenth birthday, and she looks sexy as hell, driving up with her hair blowing behind her.

"Hey, Marco! Ready to party?" She dances by me with a tank top and shorts hugging her in all the right places. I shake my head to right my foolish mind and can't even answer her. The bag of ice in my arms is suddenly melting. Her friends giggle as they pass, blatantly checkin' me out.

The party is in full swing with the booze flowing and bikini-clad bodies everywhere. There's an alcove at the lower level side door where the pool bath is located. One beer too many has me heading that way when I see her parade by in a string bikini. Mimi is backed up against the wall in the alcove with his hands all over her. His tongue is down her throat. Jimmy Bono. The guy whose been harassing her since puberty. My vision tunnels with red outlining the scene in front of me.

"Get your fucking hands off her! What did I tell you? You fuck!" I grab him by the throat and hold him up against the wall.

"Wait, Marco!" Mimi calls out. "Leave him alone, he's my boyfriend." Her petite hand with pink fingernails around my wrist.

"This guy?" One hand still pinning him and the other grasping Mimi's arm. "Seriously?"

She steps up close to me and puts her palm against my cheek. "It's okay let him go."

I roughly push him backward and storm away from everyone. Tony follows close behind out to the lakefront path. My bare feet pound the mud and stone path, and the pain doesn't even register.

"Hey bro, what happened?"

"You didn't see him with his hands all over her. He's the guy that's been getting her in trouble in school since she was seven years old. She told me things in confidence over the years. The last time was when I came back on spring break. She got suspended for kicking him in the balls after he grabbed her tit."

"Why the fuck didn't he get suspended? Did the school know he was harassing her?"

I stop and turn around to face my best friend. "They both were suspended for fighting. I fuckin went to his house, had a conversation with him, and I thought it was all over since then." I throw my hands up. "It doesn't matter anyway cause she's choosing to actually date the asshole now."

"If he hurts her, Jimmy will deal with both of us this time."

Eight

AMELIA DRAGONETTI

PRESENT-DAY

The keys to the holding room jingle from my fingers, Clyde comes running up and jumping to get to them. "Hey cutie, come here." I bend to pick him up and proceed to try and unlock the door. Turns out the keys are useless because the door is open. The holding room is where anything of value was stored when Club Beta decorated the place as a sex club. The paintings are probably worth a fortune, and Nico wants to donate them to the art museum. "Well, Clyde, we'll never know if anything was stolen cause there's no record of what's in here." He lays his head on my shoulder without a care in the world.

As soon as I open the door all the way and find the light switch, he wiggles out of my arms to investigate the new surroundings. There are stacks of dusty paintings against the walls and others hanging from them. I open the inventory document on my tablet and describe each picture. Landscapes and portraits are next to abstracts with no rhyme or reason as to the organization. I decide to categorize them into piles to more effectively inventory them.

An hour later, the paintings against the wall are in their respective labeled areas. I've photographed and cataloged each one. Clyde sits and guards the door like a good little companion. I grab the step stool to reach the art on the walls. The subject of the first, a beautiful lady dressed in Victorian fashion. When I reach up to remove it, the lady in the picture suddenly morphs into a horrifying creature with fangs for teeth and yellow eyes. The stool tips from underneath my feet when I rear backward and scream, launching me to the concrete floor. Clyde is barking like crazy as I scoop him up, hobble out of the room, face planting into Marco's solid chest.

"What happened?" His arms immediately surround the both of us in protection. I try to catch my breath and speak to no avail. "It's okay, I'm here. Try to breathe and maybe give your grip on Clyde a little slack." He transfers the terrier into his arms, not letting go of me in the process.

"It came alive… the," … breath ending in a sob, "the painting came alive and turned into a creature with big teeth and yellow eyes." A sharp pain lightning bolts through my ankle, and I slide down Marco's body to the floor. "Oh nooo!" He sets Clyde down, picks me up bridal style, and whisks me up the stairs, into the office, and onto the sofa. The little Yorkie jumps up to sit on my lap.

"You're hurt, where is the pain?" I point to my ankle, and he gently removes my boot and sock to look. "It looks sprained, but we need to get an x-ray." He rises from his knees beside me and opens the mini-fridge producing an ice pack. Gently, he places it on my ankle, then he opens his desk drawer, and out comes an ace bandage. It cleverly wraps around to keep the icepack in place.

"Maybe you should have been a doctor."

"Nah, I've just had a lot of practice with injuries when we played hockey." The side of his mouth turns up into a grin. My coat in his hands, he slips it over one arm and then the other. Once again, I'm whisked off the sofa into his arms. Outside, he places me high up on the passenger seat in his big Ram truck. I'm still wrestling with the idea of going to the ER, but my ankle is throbbing with pain. I guess it's a good idea. He runs back in and retrieves Clyde setting him in my lap before we take off for the hospital.

Nine

MARCO FIORI

Amelia's scream took about ten years off of my life. The ride to the hospital is slippery with sleet coming down from the Chicago sky. I blast the heat to warm up the car for her. Clyde is comfy inside her coat, and she's hugging him close. *Lucky pooch.*

By the time we're seen by the doctor, I wonder if I should ask him to take my blood pressure. This here is why it's better to live alone and not worry about bad things happening to people you love. Her ankle is just a bad sprain, as I predicted, and she needs to stay off it for a while. I don't see a problem with that since I love carrying her around.

"How will I be able to work? I can't just stay home. I'll go crazy!" She runs her fingers through her long hair and twists it up into a wild-looking puff on the top of her head, securing it with her handy black band.

"Don't worry, I've got you covered. I'll pick you up in the morning and drive you home at night. At the mansion, I'll carry you around. You can do things on the tablet while reclining on the sofa." I shrug, showing her it's no big deal.

"Are you crazy? I can't depend on you every day for three weeks. You're my boss!" Her eyes are wide and lips parted.

"Yes, but I'm part of the family too. Family helps each other, your mom taught me that."

She just shakes her head and stares at the floor. Clyde sticks his head out from my jacket and whines. He wants Amelia, so I place him on her lap, and she cuddles him closely. Her smile is worth everything to me, and Clyde accomplishes that.

When we arrive at the Dragonetti home, Lucia greets us in the driveway holding an umbrella with her usual reprimand of my being away too long. She shields all of us from the biting sleet raining down upon us as I carry Mimi into the house. We all file in through the front door, and Amelia wants to be put down. She steadies herself against the wall.

"That's so high up the altitude is making me dizzy. Must be nice to be so tall and be able to reach whatever you want." Her eyes roll.

My voice comes out lower than I expect. "I'll get you whatever you want, just ask."

"Marco, I've missed you! I know you're a very busy man, but everyone must make time for family." Mama D interrupts while she fluffs the pillows for her daughter.

"I know, I know, and I'm sorry. How are you? Amelia told me what happened to you."

She raises her right hand as if she's waving a fly away. "I'm fine now. It's all over, and my Anthony is happy with Elizabeth. When are you settling down? Huh?" Lucia's eyebrows rise, and she presses her lips together.

"They don't make 'em like you anymore, Mama D. I want a girl just like you, or I'm happy as a bachelor." I hug her tight.

Amelia insists on trying to walk with the crutches the hospital gave her. Her wish is my command, so I retrieve them from the car. After she's settled in on the sofa, I recline in the lazy boy next to her. Clyde settles in on my chest and snores.

"I'm messing big time with your productivity on this job. First, we go to an extended lunch, and next, we spend the afternoon in the ER." She plays with the fringe of the blanket on her lap.

"It's not a problem. I worked all night yesterday on the engineering of the pool and retractable floor. We're ahead of schedule." I raise my hand in a gesture of no big deal.

"Marco, I'm so happy you're here. You've stayed away too long. Dinner will be ready in an hour. You stay and eat with us," Mimi's mom orders from beside my chair.

"You know I wouldn't miss it, Mama D." *Just like that, I'm back in the family. Maybe it's the time, since business is booming, and I'm not dependent on them anymore.*

"Good, now I'll get you both some fresh-squeezed lemonade."

"Thanks, mom." Amelia adjusts the pillows under her foot.

Lucia returns with the drinks, an icepack under her arm for Amelia, and some frozen green beans for Clyde. His little head perks up at her offering of his favorite snack. "I'll take him in the yard to run around a bit." She takes Clyde and leaves us alone.

"Are you in any pain?" I sit up.

"No pain right now. The ice helps."

"I'll go to the pharmacy and pick up the prescription, so you have it."

"No, don't leave." She scrunches up her face. "I can take ibuprofen for pain. The Percocet gives me an upset stomach."

"Okay." I move on to the sofa next to her, put the pillow on my lap, and her ankle on top. The ice over that.

"Listen, I want to explain what happened in the holding room." I nod. "Everything was going fine. I took pictures and cataloged all the art on the floor. Then I used the step stool to reach the first one on the wall. It was a beautiful woman dressed in a Victorian gown. I photographed it first with my phone. Then when I reached up to grab it, the picture morphed into a horrifying creature with sharp teeth and yellow eyes. It lunged toward me, and I jumped back off the stool." Tears fill her eyes. "It was so real and unexpected."

"You don't have to talk about it. As long as you're okay, that's all that matters." I pat her shin.

"You don't believe me... wait, get my phone. The picture must be on there." She stirs in her seat.

"I believe you, Amelia, there's no reason not to." I lean forward and put my hand over hers. "Where's your phone?"

"I must have left it in the car." She points toward the driveway, and I go out after her phone.

Someone's fucking with us. I'm gonna find out who. When someone I care about gets hurt, there's no stopping me. Her phone is right where she left it on the seat of my car. The picture of the lady is the last one on the roll, just as she described.

Ten

TONY DRAGONETTI

THE SUN IS SETTING behind us when I pull into my parents' driveway. The clouds parted for a little while, giving us a reprieve from the freezing rain. Marco is standing next to his truck, looking at his phone. Liz and I get out of the car and greet him.

"I thought I wouldn't see you until next week's poker game." I slam my car door and walk over to him.

He puts his arm around my shoulders. "The first one since your hospital stay. How you feeling after propelling into a brick wall at breakneck speed? Do ya think you're a superhero, my man?"

"Almost back to normal. Still doing therapy for my arm. Far from a superhero, that's for sure. We're just glad all that drama is behind us now." I smile at Liz, and she nods while helping Tess out of the back seat.

"Yeah, well, I'm staying for dinner, and we'll fill you in on the drama at the mansion today. Let's go inside," Marco says.

Tess hops out and cheers. "Clyde too? Uncle Marco?" She runs to him, and he picks her up for a kiss.

"Yes, sweetie, Nana has him in the backyard under the canopy." Marco lets her down gently, and she runs up the stairs disappearing into the house. We all follow into the family room.

My little sister with a sprained ankle is on the sofa. "What the hell happened?"

Mimi tells me the whole day in detail, and I just shake my head. That place is cursed. But there has to be an explanation for what she saw.

"Hey, bro, come out into the yard with me." I follow Marco outside and leave Liz and Mimi with their heads together. Mom takes Tess inside to help set the table.

"There has to be someone fucking with us," Marco says.

"I was just thinking the same thing inside. That place is cursed, with all the shit that went on behind the scenes, while it was Club Beta. But there has to be a logical explanation for this."

"I didn't have the time to investigate because all I could think about was getting Amelia to the hospital." He scrapes his fingers through his hair.

"Let's go back after dinner and check it out. When I was posing as a client to rescue Liz, cameras were everywhere. Are they still there?"

"Yeah, but disconnected. Great idea, let's catch this asshole red-handed." He pats me on the shoulder, and we go in for dinner.

———

After my mom feeds all of us and dessert is over, we leave the girls to clean up and go to the club.

Marco unlocks the door, and we head straight for the holding room where Mimi saw the haunted painting. He holds up the picture she took of it, comparing it to all the framed art in the room.

"I don't understand. There isn't even a painting close to this one." Marco holds his arms out.

"Well, the fact that my sister has a photo of it means she's not losing her mind." I flip through some canvases against the wall.

"No, I never thought that for a minute. I believed Amelia from the minute she fell into me in the hallway." He sighs.

His face is scrunched with a worried swipe over his chin. It feels like he wants to tell me more. I've known him all my life, and we're like brothers. He speaks to me more about personal stuff than anyone.

"Let's get the cameras running, and maybe they will catch something in the next few days to explain all this weirdness."

"I'm there with ya, and maybe we should inform Nico and Sam too."

Eleven

MIMI DRAGONETTI

A WEEK HAS GONE BY QUICKLY since the incident in the holding room. Weird things have still been happening to only me. One day, while sorting photos of inventory in the office, and Marco was in the bathroom. I heard something in the hall and rolled over in my chair to look. No one was there, but it smelled strongly of cigarette smoke. Things show up on my desk in the morning like flowers, hair clips, and hard candy. The cameras have shown up with nothing. Whoever's pranking me knows how to avoid the cameras.

Marco hasn't left my side when he can help it. He carries me everywhere, refusing to let the crutches chafe my underarms. Today, he's meeting with the owner of the previous job for a walkthrough and asked his foreman Bruce to be here with me. I feel kinda silly that I need a babysitter here at the mansion. I can't wait until next week when the whole crew moves to this location, and I can hang with Kimber.

"Mimi, how you doing in here today?" Bruce asks, walking by from the main room. He uses the door jamb like a drum, his fingers beating out a tune known only in his head.

"I'm fine, lots of work to catalog all the items in this place and box them up. But we are making good progress."

"Glad to hear it." The beat continues during the pause, and it's obvious he wants something. "Listen, I'm finished with the guy marking off the dig lines for the pool. You'll be okay here alone if I go to lunch?" He scratches his head with one hand and pulls up his pants with the other.

"Sure, go ahead." I wave my hand in the air to make it more convincing, even though I'm not certain at all. I hear the side door close, and the office is eerily quiet so, I turn on the wireless speaker and bring up my playlist. I wheel myself in the office chair over to Marco's credenza and start pulling the files on my list. The picture of me as a baby in Marco's lap catches my attention. His face is pure joy, and he's holding me like a precious gift.

A feeling of being watched comes over me, and I wonder if it's because I'm alone with the cameras on.

"Hey, you the receptionist?"

I'm so startled that I swivel around in the chair and shriek. My heart is beating out of my chest. Terror replaces the warm feeling from the photograph. By the time I catch my breath to answer him, he's standing next to me.

"How did you get in here?" Somehow the letter opener ends up in my hand.

"Whoa, whoa! You scare easy! Put the weapon down, I'm not dangerous most of the time." He grabs my wrist and pries the letter opener out of my fingers, placing it on the desk. I roll backward away from him until I hit the wall. He leans his butt against Marco's desk and crosses his legs at the ankle. A cocky chuckle comes from deep in his throat as he takes a cigarette out and tilts his head to light it. The Zippo has the United States Military on the side. In that second, I size him up. Chin length dark hair with a short beard on a chiseled face, full lips, and bright blue eyes. Black leather jacket, tight straight leg jeans, and combat boots. "You got a voice? Or you just gonna sit there checkin me out? Not that I mind a hot lady like you giving me undivided attention."

"Listen, you shouldn't be here. This is private property. Please leave."

He blows smoke through his nose. "Honey, this is gonna be my home in a few months I thought I'd check it out and look who I found. A hot chick with a broken leg."

"How old are you?

"Just turned sixteen, but I know the beard makes me look twenty-two." He smirks, running his fingers over his beard.

"You're one of the kids moving here with Nico and Samantha?"

"I'm no kid, I've seen more violence, had more sex, and have done more drugs than you'll probably see in your lifetime, sweetheart." He holds his cigarette between his thumb and forefinger, bringing it up to his plump lips. "But since I'm not legal age yet with no parents, here is where they're sending me."

"Well, even if this will be where you live soon, you are not allowed to enter at will now. How did you get in?" My fingers are grasping the arms of the chair so hard they ache.

He puts his butt out in an empty can of soda that Marco left on his desk. "The door to the underground garage sticks and gets left open all the time."

"So, you been in here before?" I can hear the high-pitched tone in my voice. He shrugs his shoulders as an answer.

"I need you to leave now. I have to get back to work, and you're messing up my schedule."

He puts both hands up, palms facing me. "I'll leave now, but I just have to say one thing to you, Amelia." He grins.

"How do you know my name?" My chair is pushed so hard to the wall it will need to be repainted.

"I'm gonna know everything about you one day," he says, looking back at me from the doorway. And then he disappears.

Twelve

MARCO FIORI

AMELIA'S VOICE is shrill on the phone describing the guy that walked in on her at the mansion. My foot presses down on the gas pedal in hopes of getting to her quicker. After weaving around traffic I arrive at the mansion in record time.

"I'm so glad you're here." She hugs me from her seated position in the office chair. I kneel in front of her. Her eyes are wide as they meet mine.

"Who is this guy? Did he say his name?"

She's looking me up and down. "You have a suit on."

"I always wear a suit to walkthroughs and didn't want to waste time getting here to change."

"Get up you'll get the pants dirty." She pulls on my bicep as if she can lift me up. I chuckle at the notion and rise to my feet.

"Amelia, did he say his name?" That came out a little loud.

"No, he just said he's gonna live here when it's finished." She leans forward, brows pinched between her fingers.

I can feel the anger inside me roar to the surface, and I'm losing the battle to keep cool. "So, he's a foster kid. First, I'll call Nico and get a list of the boys moving in here. Then, Bruce is going to get a piece of my mind for leaving you alone." I sit at my desk and fish my phone out of my pocket.

"No! Please, Marco. I told him he could get lunch." I stop and look up at her. Her face is scrunched with the pleas. "I feel stupid even getting you all riled up about this. Please don't embarrass me in front of the crew."

"Well, the least he can do is fix the door to the underground garage."

"Yes, that's a great idea." She nods enthusiastically.

I dial Nico, and he answers on the second ring. "Hey buddy, does Samantha have a list of the kids moving in here yet?"

"Yeah, some of them, why?"

I hear Sam in the background asking what's wrong.

"Can she look to see if there's a sixteen-year-old boy on there? A kid walked in here today and said he was moving in soon. I need to know who this kid is." The pencil I'm holding doesn't have a chance as I wait.

"She's looking right now. There's nobody sixteen on the list yet. Sam says the judges are still populating the list from new cases. Hey, did this kid do something?"

"Nothing against the law except trespassing, but I don't like Amelia here alone with this kid getting in. Don't worry I'll handle it. It's my job to keep my workers safe."

"Okay, man, if you need me, I'm always here."

"Thanks." I hang up and call Bruce to get the door fixed as soon as he gets back.

Thirteen

MIMI DRAGONETTI

IT FEELS as if I'm overreacting. But since I'm unable to run, and stuck in the chair, I felt trapped. He was just a sixteen-year-old boy… who was at least six feet, *and* had a beard. When Marco walks in, all my fears evaporate. It must be his sheer size. When he holds me, there's nothing that could ever hurt me. My whole body is engulfed with warmth. The memory of how that felt when I was a child comes rushing back. He kneels at my feet, and when I look into his eyes, they blaze with powerful intensity. His eyebrows are so scrunched together, premature wrinkles are a possibility. I persuade him to get off his knees, and when he stands, broad shoulders and muscular thighs cannot be contained by the expensive suit he wears. He takes up so much room in our little office that I can't see around him. I force myself to push down the sudden longing in my body. *He thinks of me as a sister. Stop it, Mimi.*

After he makes two calls, Marco removes his suit jacket and sits in front of his computer. "I want to show you something. Slide on over here."

Gladly, I roll my little office chair up next to him. His long fingers clack over the keys to reveal a website called Undead Portraits with the painting of the lady I saw in the holding room. When he presses the arrow, the exact scene I witnessed plays on the monitor.

"That's the portrait I saw! You found it." I point to the screen.

"This is how it was accomplished, but now we need to find out who set you up as the unknowing victim. This is why the painting was gone when Tony and I returned."

"They put a frame around a television. No wonder it was attached to the wall. The dim lighting in the holding room made it undetectable. Marco, thank you for believing me." I kiss him on the cheek taking in his scent of sandalwood and seawater.

Marco surprises me when his hands caress my face. "I was so afraid for you here alone. This is a sick childish joke."

Deep soulful brown eyes disappear behind his lids as he brings my lips to his. He gently rubs them against mine, enough to taste wintergreen. I bravely deepen the kiss, crawling onto his lap. Our tongues, teeth, and lips, exploring for the first time. My fingers lace themselves into the hair at his nape, and his arms tighten around my waist. Just like that …the world disappears. The man kisses like he's a thirsty traveler in the desert and just found the only source of water. Our chests are heaving bodies crushed together when he pulls his lips from mine. Forehead to forehead, his right-hand caresses my cheek, slowly rubbing the pad of his thumb over my bottom lip.

"We can't do this, Meems."

Finally, he calls me by the nickname he used to when we were younger. I didn't know until now just how much I'd craved that.

"Why not?" My eyes never leave his lips, so close to mine. I can feel his breath.

"Because your brother is my best friend… Because I'm too old for you… Because your parents have loved me as if I was their own for almost my whole life… They trust me with you… They know I want what's best for you." The tone of his voice raises with every reason.

"Maybe you're what's best for me?" I whisper.

As if I weigh nothing, he picks me up into his arms while standing up and gently sits me on his desk. His fingers run through his hair, pulling it in all directions as he paces.

"Fuck! I'm not strong enough to stop myself when it comes to you."

"There's no need to stop. We're both consenting adults." I can't ignore the feeling in my belly.

"It's not possible Amelia, I'm sorry." Hands clenched into fists, he heads out of the office.

I wrap my arms around myself. Protection from the chill his absence leaves.

Fourteen

MARCO FIORI

CHI-TOWN WEATHER IS clear and crisp, with warming sunshine coming through my window. You can't let it fool you, though, because as soon as you go out the door, the wind chill gets you. The streets are melting, leaving behind wet asphalt spitting at my windshield.

Clyde looks up at me from the harness in the front seat next to me. "I know, buddy, this is a mess. But I want you to be the buffer between us today. Keep her busy." He tilts his head to one side and then to the other, his ears on full alert. I exit on my side and go around to unhook Clyde. Amelia's car is already here because today is the first day she drove here herself. I didn't like it but understood it was for the best.

"Hey, Clyde!" She hobbles over to us and takes him from my arms without a word to me. She looks tired and cuddles Clyde longer and tighter than usual.

"How's the ankle today? It must be better since you insisted on driving yourself this morning."

"I'm fine." Her lips press together in a quick pink slash making her eyes squint.

"The men are coming with the mini backhoe today to dig the pool. Can you make sure Clyde stays in here with you?"

She kisses Clyde on the head and nods. Then hobbles over to where his bed is under my desk. She picks it up in her other hand and sets it next to her chair. Clyde snuggles in, right next to her feet, and she opens her laptop without another word. *I would have brought her the dog bed if she asked.*

I settle in behind my desk, trying not to look up at her across from me. The silence is deafening except for the clickity-clack of her fingers on the keys.

"You want to sign off on the tile order? I can get it by the deadline."

"Sure." I rise and walk over to her desk to sign. She smells like vanilla and lavender. Her eyes look up at me without moving her head. *Crap, she knows I was breathing her in.* "How about Chinese food for lunch today?"

"Marco, you don't have to buy me lunch every day," She huffs.

"Maybe I want to," I smirk, looking down at her.

"You could have lunch with any girl you choose. Why waste time eating with me?" Her tone is slightly argumentative. But I keep my voice low and pleasant.

"I like your company. Spending time with you is never a waste."

She rolls her eyes and starts clacking again on her computer. I reluctantly pull myself away and back to my seat. Someone pounds on the outside door, and I leave to answer it. Must be the machine operator.

Fifteen

MIMI DRAGONETTI

MARCO IS out in the big room directing the machine operator on the pool dig. He's been out of our office all day after he brought me Chinese food for lunch. We ate across from each other in silence. It's fine, I have nothing to say after he rejected me the other day. I was pissed at first now, I just feel empty and awkward.

Clyde's little nub of a tail wags as I hand him over to him. There's too much noise to talk to him, so I simply gesture that I'm leaving for the day. When I walk outside, the sun is setting, and traffic is loud. In the parking lot, I unlock my car. Still limping slightly, I head in that direction.

"Amelia, wait up."

I turn to find the same guy that was in my office smoking a cigarette. His blue eyes catch the setting sunlight with an arresting sparkle. Damn, he looks so much older than his sixteen years. He says goodbye to the other guys he's with and heads over to me. Now that I'm standing next to him, he's much taller than my five-foot-four frame. He runs his fingers through his chin-length hair and smiles at me. For some reason, outside in the sunlight, he's not as imposing as I thought. He holds out his hand to shake mine.

"I realized I never introduced myself. I'm Alex Greyson."

I shake and give him a closed-mouth smile, sizing him up.

"Look, I apologize for startling you the other day. Can we start over?" His eyebrows are raised, and that eye twinkle is intense.

His face is so innocent and charming I find myself grinning back at him.

"What are you doing here again?" I lean on my one good ankle and place my hand on a nearby car for balance. He moves in closer and leans on the car as well, almost too flirty.

He lifts one shoulder and both eyebrows in reply. "This's a great place to hang when I'm not creating."

"Creating what exactly?" I tilt my head.

"I got a whole set up at my buddy's house. I'm a photographer and videographer." He smiles, proud of his declaration.

I could feel him study me, his assessment making me feel like a project he needs to finish. "That's great, listen, I gotta go." I balance my weight on both feet gingerly.

He laughs through his nose, but the sound is constricted. "You still scared of me?" He puts his hands out to his sides, palms facing me.

"No, I just need to leave. See ya around." My reflection in the car window is tight. I force myself to soften it with a small smile and a waggle of my fingers as I get into my car. When I look back to pull out of the space, he's gone.

My mom must have pot roast cooking for dinner. It smells divine.

"How's the ankle? Elizabeth asks when I hobble into the kitchen.

"Walking on it all day has made me wish for an ice pack." I sigh, blowing air out forcefully.

"Sit, I'll get it for you." She opens the freezer. I prop my leg on the chair, and she sets the ice on my ankle before sitting down.

"The sister I always wished for and never had is finally here," I giggle.

"Same here." She gives my hand a squeeze. "What's going on at the mansion today?" She crosses her legs.

"They're digging the pool today." I circle my head, stretching my neck.

"What else? I can always tell when you're stressed. How about a glass of wine?" She gets up to fetch my dad's Cabernet Sauvignon.

I'm so glad my brother and Liz are back together. She genuinely cares and loves our family. Tony is a different person now that they are finally together.

After taking a sip, I confide in my older best friend/ almost sister-in-law. "I don't know what to do about Marco. I think I'm starting to develop feelings for him."

"Wow, that's great! How do you think he feels about you?"

Sigh. "Why is it great? My brothers and my parents will never approve of our age gap. And he told me it could never happen."

"What! Why? Does he know you're a virgin?" She whispers the last word. "When did you discuss a relationship with him? Tell me everything."

My eyes scan the ceiling. "How would he know that? It's not like I walk around with a scarlet V on my chest." I rub my lips together and continue. "He kissed me. Then I crawled into his lap and kissed him harder." Liz's eyebrows raise into her hairline. "Afterward, he stood and put me down. Then gave me three reasons we can never be together. Number one, Tony is his best friend." I count off with my fingers in the air. "Number two, Mom and Dad trust him. Number three, he's too old for me."

"He is not too old for you! Look at your brother and me we're five years apart."

"Yeah, but we're almost seven." I blow out a breath between pierced lips. "Like I need this right now with all the other decisions I have."

She holds up three fingers. "Number one, Tony loves Marco like a brother, and I know he would be happy that you would be with someone so mature, loving, and protective. Not to mention the guy owns a great business, and money will never be a problem." One finger goes down. "Number two, Mom and Dad are crazy about him and already love him as their own. Dad even helped him when he started his business." Another disappears. "Number three, you'll be happier with an older man who's already dated around and is ready to be a one-woman man. It's difficult to find that in a guy, they all just want sex." Her index finger stays up and pokes me in the shoulder. "Number four, the man is hot as Hades on a summer day. From toe to tip, he's man candy waiting to be enjoyed."

We both crack up, and I nod enthusiastically. "The girls in his office call it the Fiori fantasy." I feel my cheeks heat.

"Oh, yeah, believe me, I get it." She fans herself and giggles.

Sixteen

MARCO FIORI

THE GUYS ARE GETTING an early morning start putting in the rebar for the shape of the pool. Next, they blow in the medium that dries into a finished Olympic size swimming pool. By the time Amelia arrives, they're smoothing it all to a fine finish. Clyde jumps up, and she scoops him into her arms. *Lucky pooch.*

"Good morning." I sit in my desk chair and lean back.

"Morning, are you going to the Halloween gala?"

"Yeah, it's for a good cause so, I'm in. Not fond of the mandatory costume rule."

She shrugs and sits at her desk. "I like getting all dressed up for Halloween. You probably think it's juvenile." Her lips press together, and she shakes her head.

"I've been to a few costume events even when I was your age. I've always hated dressing up." I speak without thinking. *Damn!*

"Oooh, even when you were my age!" She stands, placing Clyde in his bed, and puts her hands on her hips. Her cute little pink lips scrunched up. "You know Tony and Liz are five years apart in age. And so are Sam and Nico." She plants her perfect ass on my desk, crossing her legs. "Why are you so hung up on that?"

I compose myself and try with all my willpower to forget how much I want her. She has on tight leggings with ankle boots and a long filmy blouse over them. Her brown, silky hair is loose over her shoulders, and when my gaze reaches higher, she stares into my eyes with huge olive-shaped ones framed in wisps of lashes. "I can see we need to talk about this." I get up and close the office door and lock it. Then sit back down, letting out a forceful sigh. "I had just turned seven years old when one day Tony and I were playing in the treehouse in your parents' backyard. Your dad opened the slider and yelled for us to come into the house. We scrambled down the ladder. Once inside, he made both of us wash our hands at the laundry room sink and dry them well. Then he led us into the family room, where your mom sat in the rocking chair with her back to us. It was eerily quiet even though Daniel and Dominic were standing there too. Tony ran ahead of me into the room and rounded the chair with his eyes as big as saucers.

Your mother turned her head to look back at me and said, "Marco, come see her, don't be afraid to join us." She always made me feel like part of your family and still does." Amelia puts her hand over mine on the desk and squeezes. "Anyway, I peeked over her shoulder, getting my first glimpse of *you* in her arms. You were small and pink with big eyes and long eyelashes." Amelia smiles. "The only way I can describe how I felt at that moment is like a time-lapse video of a flower leaning toward the sun, its petals opening and filling the world with color. That was my heart in my chest, revealing to me a rush of feelings I never experienced before towards another human being. To fiercely protect and cherish you is all I could think about."

Amelia hops down from the desk takes both of my hands into her own spreading them so she can crawl into my lap. I shouldn't let her but what I told her is so intimate it seems appropriate. She lays her head against my shoulder, and we stay there quietly for a minute.

"What you just told me further cements the fact that we should attempt a relationship." I smile in response and place a kiss on her forehead. "Why are you holding back, Marco?"

"Believe me, it hasn't been easy." I bring up her chin to look me in the eye. "But I made a promise to always protect you from heartache and harm. A relationship with me would only bring you heartache. It's been evident to me in the past few years that I should remain alone."

Seventeen

MIMI

THE FALL COLORS have outdone previous years in Chi-town. As I drive back from shopping on Michigan Avenue, the trees take on a life of their own. Breezes coming through my window smell like autumn, and the houses are decked out in outrageous Halloween decorations. It seems the affluent neighborhoods along Sheridan road waste no expense celebrating the seasons.

The dressmaker had me try on my costume one last time before the party tonight. It was perfect! I only wish I could tell someone about it, but a stipulation in the invitations was to keep costumes a secret. Probably more fun that way.

"Hey, mom, what's for dinner?" The garage door squeaks to a close behind me as I walk into the kitchen, toting all my bags.

"Chicken parmesan," she turns from the oven. "Did you get your costume?"

"Yup. You will have to wait and see when I'm all dressed."

"Okay, honey. Dinner is in ten." She turns to stir the gravy.

I place all the pieces of my outfit on my bed and jump in the shower. After dinner, I'm almost finished with my makeup and hair when my mom knocks.

"Come in." I stand and give her the full effect of the costume.

"Hey, sweetie, wow, you look amazing! Just like Kate Beckinsale in Van Helsing!"

"That's the look I was going for." I hug her.

"You're even prettier." She steps back for another look, still holding my hands.

I roll my eyes and reply. "You have to say that. You're my mom. Hehe."

"The costume is a replica of the one in the movie."

"Yeah, I like it because it's sexy without showing lots of skin." I admire myself in the mirror.

"Is there someone playing Hugh Jackman's part tonight?" She grins.

"Mom! No, not this time." My mind goes back to the story Marco told me a few days ago, wishing it could be him.

"Have a great time sweetie, I'll see you in the morning. Love you."

"Love you too, mom."

"Wow, you look just like that vampire slayer in Van Helsing." The skeleton doorman at the entrance proclaims over the creepy organ music in the background.

"Thanks!" I giggle as I slide by him into the gala. Liz and Tony have done a great job decorating the old Victorian house for Halloween. All the work Tony put in the past year updating it has faded to the background in favor of the spooky holiday. The fog machines create a mist at floor level, while the black fabrics and spider webs create a ghoulish vibe. The guests have all seemed to favor the macabre costumes this year over the silly or playful.

"Wow, sis, you look awesome. Kate had nothing on you," Tony says, planting a kiss on my cheek from behind. When I turn, laughter overcomes me to see my brother dressed as Gomez Addams. My eyes even begin to tear when Liz comes up behind him as Morticia, trying to walk in the tight black gown with the tails dragging on the floor.

THE DELETED HEIR 59

"You two a-are cra-cking me up." I hold my stomach, bending over. Liz's long black wig hits me in the mouth when she hugs me hello.

"We're the Addams family! Wait till you see Tess as Wednesday. She's around here somewhere."

"Love it!"

"Come to the bar, Sam and Jen are already two drinks ahead." She drags me into the living room with her spikey nailed hand in mine. "Gomez, make us some drinks!"

I put my sword on the bar and greet the others. Jennifer is a zombie pirate with her handsome Jaxson dressed similarly. From under his flamboyant hat, I can see Jaxson's beard is grown out more than usual, with the blood of his victims dripping off. They both have rings on every finger, and leather boots Jen's are thigh-high. The bows of her garter peek out from under the almost nonexistent skirt to finish off the look.

"Hey, Mimi, you want tequila or vodka?" My brother yells from behind the bar.

"Margarita on the rocks, please."

"Wait until you see Samantha and Nico," Jen whispers. "Turn around here they come."

Samantha is leading Nico with his huge green hand. He appears to be seven feet tall on shoes that look like bricks. His ripped shirt shows muscular green biceps and chest. I've never seen a sexier Frankenstein all the way up to the bolts on his neck. He bends at the waist to place a kiss on my cheek.

"You look beautiful, Mimi."

"Thank you. You look scary and sexy all at once. Not sure how it can, but I know Sam's a lucky girl."

"Don't I know it!" Samantha moves in for a hug. My mouth hangs open at the height of her black hair with white lightning bolt streaks. Her face is white, and her lips a pouty red. Her white gown is cut low to her waist and frayed at the edges.

"How did you fit in the car with the hair?"

"NOT easy. I had to put the seat completely down." We both break out in a fit of giggles. "People were staring not because of his costume, but Nico looked like he was talking to himself. I was reclined, out of sight."

My brother Dominic slinks up behind Sam and kisses her cheek. "All my favorite women in one place. I'm so lucky."

"What about Mom?" I tease.

"She's number one." He hugs me and kisses my cheek. Zombie blood sticks to my face, and I swipe at it.

"Watch out with the fake blood, Dom."

"Taste it. Daniel made it with ingredients from Mom's kitchen." He licks his lips.

I lick my finger, tasting sweetness. "Mmm, what's in it?"

"Ask him, zombie surgeon is right behind you." Dominic gestures with his chin.

Daniel is there in his surgical scrubs with a zombie nurse on his arm. I cannot even look at what he has on until I digest the nurse's get up. She leaves nothing to the imagination as to what her nipples look like under the sheer, short dress. Her body is bangin' and warrants even a slight girl crush. Daniel lets her go for a second to hug me. "You look amazing sis."

Tony bumps elbows to greet Daniel, his hands full, with drinks. The place is crowded, with me in the middle of the circle. Between seven-foot-tall Frankenstein, his bride's skyscraper do, and the pirate hats big as umbrellas, claustrophobia is setting in. I finagle around everyone to a clear spot and take a deep breath, but all the oxygen leaves the room at the sight of *him*.

Marco Fiori is the epitome of my fantasy. Kimber was psychic. He leans against the door jamb at the entrance to the room, talking to Liz. The gods have aligned in such a way that our costumes are a complementary pair. Neither one of us knew what the other would be wearing, but we fit together like puzzle pieces. I dressed as the vampire slayer, he dressed for the slaying. Long black leather coat over a silver vest, an ascot, gracing his masculine throat. Thick, shiny hair combed back from his beautiful face with blood artistically dripping from his sensual lips. When he smiles at Morticia, the sharp canine teeth peek through to make the whole ensemble frighteningly sexy. Tonight, my proverbial slaying will do him in, so he agrees that we belong together. *My mind is certain he has no choice because I'm determined to have that man.*

Eighteen

MARCO FIORI

Liz leads me from the doorway to the bar, where everyone looks mighty enthusiastic about the holiday. Heat crawls up my body like an electrical current as soon as I zoom in on Mimi. Hugs and handshakes are coming at me from all angles, but I cannot look at anything but her. Hair falling in loose ringlets over her shoulders. Sexy leather bustier accentuating her tits that burst out through the white blouse with red stitching. Pants so tight they look painted on her curvy body. She emulates the actress in that movie. But Amelia even has her beat. When the crowd disperses, leaving us standing in front of each other, I'm at a loss for words. *She's blowing my mind.*

"Sure you want to hug the vampire slayer?" She smirks with her arms out in front of her.

I move in, placing my arms around her, burying my face in her hair. Making sure only she can hear my answer. "What an amazing way to go. You slay me every time I am in your presence." Mimi is hitting my sense of smell as intimately as all the other senses in my body.

Taking the hug to a firmer hold, she moans. Cherries are the signature scent of her hair this time. It makes my mouth water. It feels like all eyes are on us when I release her. But it's my imagination. Tony's busy with his head down behind the bar.

"You look beautiful Meems." My voice is hoarse, and I clear my throat quietly.

"Thank you. You don't look so bad yourself. Let's take a walk outside." She slides her petite little hand into mine, leading the way to the French doors out the back of the house.

"Tony did a great job renovating this place. The view alone is to die for."

She nods her head, still holding my hand on our way to the lakeshore. The sound of the water lapping against the rocks is peaceful. The moon reflecting off the water, and Mimi's silky hair makes me sigh.

"I want to discuss the possibility of us being together." She faces me, hands on her hips, her golden-brown eyes full of hope. "I know you want it too. Just what you said to me in there proves it."

That's my girl. Never afraid to say what's on her mind. So brave and yet delicate as a flower.

"Meems, there's nothing in the world I would like more." I place my hands on her shoulders. "But we can't. Tony would kill me, and I would be going against your parents' trust in me."

"We'll keep it a secret until you're ready to tell them. I'll talk to my parents myself if that's what you want." Her eyes fill with tears, and I can't bear it if she cries, but I don't know what else to say.

"No way! It's my place to tell them. But what if it doesn't work out. The last thing I ever want to do is to hurt you. I'm not an easy person to be with. Anyone I ever dated will gladly attest to that."

"Who said that?" Her tone is loud as she rolls her eyes.

"In my last relationship, she broke up with me because I didn't pay enough attention to her. She said I never talked to her and wouldn't open up."

Mimi steps closer, looking into my eyes, and rubbing her cherry lips together.

"With you and me, it's different. We've known each other all our lives." She shakes her head side to side. "You're opening up to me right now already. There are never any secrets or animosity between us, and we've worked in perfect sync every day for over two months.

What you said to me the other day proves that fate has put us together."

She puts her palms on my chest, sliding them up around my neck. On her tiptoes, she kisses me with heat and longing in her lips and body. For a moment, she pulls back, her eyes wide, and says, "The vampire teeth make it kinky." She runs her tongue over the fake pointed tooth attached to my own.

I'm only human despite what my costume portrays, and I can't push her away. Instead, my hands enclose her waist, pulling her against my body. I'm thankful we're hidden from sight when she hops up and wraps her legs around my waist. Our breathing escalates simultaneously as her nails score my scalp. The heat between her thighs mingles with my own. She breaks the kiss.

"Let's go to my house. Mom and Dad are in Lake Geneva, and there's no one there." Our foreheads smooshed together, breaths swiftly rising and falling in our chests.

"I want you. But let's go to mine."

"No, it's too far. It'll be fine. Come on."

Nineteen

MIMI DRAGONETTI

"Our house has felt empty since Tony moved into his renovated mini-mansion with Liz and Tess. Between my mom and dad spending most of their time at the house in Lake Geneva and all my brothers living on their own, I have the house to myself most of the time." Marco nods, acting just as quiet as the short ride over here. "If the ride here gave you time for second thoughts, put them out of your mind. This is happening." I push him down on the sofa and straddle his lap. Kinda getting off on being the aggressor. "You smell like leather, ocean, and masculinity." I rub my nose and lips down the side of his throat.

"What does masculinity smell like?" He laughs.

"Mmmm. Amazing." I unbutton his vest and the loose cotton shirt, palming his pecs. I can feel his erection through his tight pants, but there is no other reaction as if he's exercising complete restraint. I decide to challenge him more when I unsnap my leather bustier letting the girls free under my flimsy white blouse. He moans, white-knuckling the arm of the sofa with one hand and fisting his other. I take his fisted hand into mine, urging him to open it. Then I place a kiss on his palm and position it on my breast. Marco closes his eyes, his head falling back against the pillows. The angle of his neck turns me on, and

I begin sucking on his Adam's apple. In one fell swoop, he flips us over. The restraint has vanished like a popped bubble into thin air.

It's almost funny that today is Halloween because when Marco looks down into my eyes, it scares the crap out of me.

Vampire teeth? No.

Muscular body and neck? No.

Strong set jaw with full-blood red lips? No.

His eyes? Yup.

The full force of his longing for me is a laser beam into my soul. Time seems to stop as neither one of us moves, the mute conversation going on between us with powerful intensity.

"There's no going back if we do this Meems, are you sure?" His breaths are hot and heavy against my skin.

"Positive," I answer with a nod.

With that, he rips my blouse down the middle burying his head into my chest. With a clean-shaven jaw, he brushes back and forth over my nipples, making them erect. A moan escapes as his lips take the assault to the next level.

Marco stands, and just when I think he's going to stop us from having sex, he removes his coat and shirt then picks me up bridal style. After taking stairs two at a time with me in his arms, we fall onto my bed. I remove my arms from my shredded blouse and slide my leggings down, throwing them on the floor. When I turn to look at him, his expression is softer.

"You are exquisite, and I don't deserve you."

"You deserve everything that happens tonight and more. Come here." I grab his belt, unbuckling it, and reach in to wrap my hand around his impressive erection. My other hand unzips and sets him free, allowing me to show him how much I think he deserves with my mouth.

"Look at me…" I lift my head, and we lock gazes. "I want to make this about your pleasure now." He gently rearranges our positions, slipping my thong off. "I want to hear you whimper… make you squirm… ruin you for all other men."

Blink. Nod.

He palms my ass to elevate my body as if devouring me is his mission in life. "Oh god…" The bliss of orgasm takes over when his fingers join his talented mouth. Marco makes good on his promise multiple times. Weightless and limp afterward in his arms. He was right. No other man will do, ever.

Twenty

MIMI

Today is my brother Tony's birthday. I'm using the pizzelle iron to make him his favorite cookies. My mother bought me my iron last year for Christmas, and I'm obsessed. They are the perfect gift for any occasion, and everyone loves them. I take the chilled dough out of the frig and sit in front of the preheated iron. Measuring a spoonful of dough onto each side, I press down the cover to cook them. The process has become so second nature that I let my mind wander while I make the cookies.

Last night was amazing. Marco took my body to places it's never been before *and* without having actual intercourse. The girls were right, Marco is the Fiori Fantasy come true. The way he held me and treated me with such reverence was a turn-on in itself. After multiple orgasms, I fell gloriously asleep in his arms, our naked bodies pressed against each other.

"I smelled my favorite cookies and thought I was dreaming."

Marco jolts me out of my contemplations and makes my mouth water, just looking at him leaning against the doorframe. His bright white smile almost knocks me over. My brother Dominic's college grey sweatpants hang low on his hips, and his chiseled bare chest is on full display. It's suddenly hot in here.

"Are these your favorite too?" My voice is high and crackly, so I clear my throat before continuing. "I'm making them for my brother for his birthday."

He walks over and grabs a cookie off the plate, then takes the shaker full of powdered sugar and douses it. When he takes a bite, the sugar drops all over his chest and clings to his lips. I almost lose my shit when his masterful tongue licks it off his swollen lips. Forget fantasies. This is food porn. I can't stop myself from standing and closing the gap between us.

"You have powdered sugar on your cheek," I say, looking up at him through my eyelashes. "Oh!" The wind is knocked out of me when his arms snake around my waist, propelling my body into his.

"Lick it off, Mimi."

I zero in on the spot and move my mouth toward it when he swiftly turns his head and devours my lips instead. The kiss makes my toes curl, and lava seep into my lower belly. The sweatpants can't hide his arousal against my stomach.

"What happened to Dracula's fangs?"

"Give me your neck, no fangs necessary to put you under my spell." He sucks just below my ear. I score my nails into his scalp pulling him closer. I desire everything Marco has to offer. *Is he the one to make my first time the best it can be?*

The smell of something burning hits me, and I break the kiss to flip open the iron, revealing two dark brown burnt cookies. Marco chuckles, and I shake my head.

"Sorry, I couldn't help myself when I saw you there in your little shorts and tank top. This pint-size domestic diva, baking my favorite cookies. The sight was like food porn."

I laugh at his description and how he must have read my mind. "Well, Mr. Fiori, the girls at the office were right." The smirk on his face and the lust in his eyes melt my brain.

"What did they say?" He pulls out the plug of the pizzelle iron.

"They've nicknamed you the Fiori Fantasy." I pick up the sugar and shake it out all over his chest. He bends and picks me up like I weigh nothing.

"They did, did they? Well, you're the *only one* I'm going to turn fantasy into reality with, *right now*."

Twenty-One

MARCO FIORI

LAKESHORE DRIVE IS bumper to bumper while my mind wanders to the forbidden time I spent with Amelia last night and this morning. Her body is so responsive, but I could tell she's inexperienced. Maybe, even still a virgin. The way she tried to take control was hot, and I was helplessly succumbing to her charms against whatever restraint I tried to muster. It can't happen again. Next time, I might not be able to hold back. If she's a virgin, she should be with a man that can give her a long-term relationship. Thoughts of another man's hands on her ache in my chest. I turn on the radio to get my mind off of it. A book on tape loads automatically at the part I left off. I allow my thoughts to absorb the author's wisdom about the death of a sibling. Books on tape or podcasts are my favorite way to pass the time in traffic.

The author, Kady Braswell, describes the loss of a sibling and how it means losing a part of yourself. Quotes from her podcast enlighten me as to how I felt when my little sister drowned.

"It's like a limb amputation. That's not a wound someone can ever heal from; it's one you must learn to function despite it."

"The halo of childhood, that feeling of being untouchable, is destroyed in the face of a sibling's death."

"A harmful thought may recur: *They died because I failed to* *protect them.* **Often, this is completely untrue, but overcoming guilt and realizing you are not to blame is part of the healing process."**

There it is. That's my nightmare. I could have saved my sister if I hadn't stayed after school with my friends. I failed to protect my baby sister; therefore, I don't deserve to be happy. I can only imagine how my mother felt before she took her own life immersed in grief.

The parking lot is crowded at the mansion since my other employees have joined us. Kimber waves as she exits her car and unlocks the side door. I stay in my car for a few moments to get my head straight. Do the breathing exercises the doctor taught me. The book on tape and the feelings it drew to the surface are neatly packed back up and compartmentalized by the time I exit my truck. Work-related thoughts are now my focus, and I can go into the job ready to lead my staff.

"Marco, the pool looks amazing!" Kimber is standing at the edge, admiring the blue water chomping on her usual stick of gum. She's so young and unaffected by the world's trials and tribulations. Just like Amelia when she was in high school. Surprisingly, it makes the difference stand out to me. *Mimi is so much more mature now.*

"Wait till everyone sees how the retractable floor works. When Nico and Sam come for the walkthrough, I'll unveil it." I'm kind of proud of myself for taking in the feat of engineering.

"The guys have already started on the lower level. The plans for the bedrooms look fun for the kids." She claps her hands together and jumps up and down, causing her ponytail to bounce. Kimber is still a kid herself in many ways, but she is a fast learner and has a responsible work ethic.

"Yeah, what Samantha is creating here is amazing. Some unlucky kids will find some luck in life while living here."

"It's beautiful." She beams at me.

I gesture with my chin in the direction of her office. "Come on, let's get the orders in so we can finish on schedule."

"Slave driver." She lifts her hand as if cracking a whip. "Ca... chew." Then making the sound.

We both laugh and walk side by side to the offices. I always kid around with Kimber by resting my arm on the top of her head. She's the perfect height for it.

Amelia is at her desk looking gorgeous as usual. "Where's Clyde? I thought you would stop and pick him up to bring him since he was alone all night." Her cheeks are pink enough to match her tight little sweater. My mind wanders to last night and how she looks under it, delaying my answer a few seconds. "Marco?"

I clear my mind and my throat. "I texted my landlord to go in and feed him last night. She wants to keep him today." I round my desk and sit leaning back in my chair. I'd thought I could have the talk with Mimi about last night being a one-time thing, but the words are stuck in my throat.

Twenty-Two

AMELIA

KIMBER IS on the phone when I enter her office. Without Clyde here and Marco leaving early for the day, I'm lonely. Her extra-long fingernails click on the keyboard. She gestures with her head for me to have a seat. When she hangs up and walks around the desk, I envy her long legs and tight figure. Girls like her always look older and can pull off fake IDs in college. My five-foot-three curvy figure and huge eyes make me look younger. Getting into drinking establishments before I was twenty-one was difficult sometimes. The bouncer looks extra-long at my ID now and shakes their head.

"How's it goin' Mimi?" She cracks her gum and twists her ponytail around her fist.

"We haven't had time to go to lunch or even talk, we have been so busy lately." I shrug.

"Marco wants to have as much cosmetic stuff done before the unveiling of the pool to the Pope's right before Christmas. I'm in charge of the orders getting here on time."

"Will the lower level be finished? It's still a wreck down there."

"No, just the main floor and most of the Pope's living quarters. Samantha will put the final changes on that very soon. The lower level will be last to be completed." Her fingers wipe the dust off the stapler.

"Yeah, I thought so. What did you do for Halloween? Anything exciting?"

"My friends and I watched scary movies and ate popcorn." This girl loves bubblegum. She blows a bubble and pops it.

"I loved doing that when I was still in school." I sit back in the chair and get more comfortable.

"I graduated in June but haven't decided if I'm going to college." She removes the band on her pony and slides it on her wrist, then runs her fingers through her long blond hair.

"I'm kinda in the same boat, but I went to college and still don't know what I want to do. It's so friggin hard trying to figure out what I want to do for the rest of my life."

"I hear ya. That's why I'm working here. Gettin' a feel for what it's like to work in an office. At first, I thought it would be boring and claustrophobic, but we move around so much it's actually great. Marco's taught me so much about running a business that I'm kicking around the idea of being a general contractor."

"That's great if you already have a plan. I think I want to be an interior designer." I look up at the ceiling and exhale forcefully.

"Have you researched any part of what it takes to become one?" Her head tilts to the side.

"I've applied to three different schools, The International Academy of Art and Design and Harrington here in Chicago, and The American Institute of Interior Design in Arizona."

"Wow, I would love to move to a warm climate..."

"Hi, is Marco around?" I turn in my chair toward the voice and find a petite brunette with red lips and false eyelashes. She looks me up and down without a sensor, so I do the same to her. This one's dressed to impress a man. *My man.* Her bodycon short dress skims smoothly over her voluptuous curves. The nails on her small hands are manicured to smooth perfection, as is her hair. She has on a leather moto jacket with ankle boots.

"Hi Caitlin, he's gone for today. I can tell him you were here... Um, why don't you just call him?" Kimber asks, her expression widens.

The brunette's eyes turn from me to Kimber, giving her a condescending closed-mouth smile. "We had a disagreement, and I wanted to speak to him. I'll come back tomorrow." She inspects her nails and pauses. "Do me a favor and don't tell him I was here. I want to surprise him."

"You got it." Kimber gives her a thumbs up, and the woman disappears down the hallway.

Pushing herself off from leaning on the edge of the desk, she quietly closes the door.

"That was weird. Caitlin and Marco have been..." she uses her fingers as air quotes. "seeing each other for a while now."

"Oh really?" I can feel my blood boiling over inside of me. But I have to make off like nothing is wrong. "How serious is it?"

Kimber sits back behind her desk, rearranging papers. "I think she's tons more serious than he is. He avoids her calls regularly and rolls his eyes behind her back when she's nagging him. Most of the time, when she comes to see him at work, he gets her out as soon as he possibly can, and if she refuses, he blatantly ignores her until she leaves." Another bubble and pop.

"Interesting, I never pegged Marco for being outright rude to anyone."

"She's pretty forward and fake most of the time. I never understood what he sees in her. I think she brings out the worst in him." Kimber shrugs.

When I leave Kimber's office, Alex Greyson is waiting for me outside the front door under the canopy. He's got on skinny jeans with a ripped leather jacket over a t-shirt and his signature combat boots.

"Hey, how's it goin'?" He's smoking his signature cigarette, squeezing it between his thumb and forefinger, flicking it across the lot.

"Why are you stalking me? Was it you that left that stuff on my desk?" I stand up straighter.

"Did you like it?" He shifts on his feet.

"I asked you a question, please answer, or I'm leaving." My hands are on my hips, and I'm inwardly embarrassed at my old lady demeanor. But he did frighten me the first time we met.

He runs his fingers through his chin-length hair and looks out into the parking lot. "Okay, I guess you deserve an explanation. But promise you won't be mad at me."

"I won't promise you anything." I lift my chin, shaking my head.

"Can we sit in your car where it's warm? This might take a few minutes." The crease between his eyebrows deepen.

"No, here, come back inside." I unlock the door and hold it open, waving him inside.

He paces the hallway before beginning his speech. "At first, I knew you were Tony Dragonetti's sister, and I wanted to show you what I could do with photography and video. You know… so… you could get me a job at your family's company." He's reluctant to look me in the eye. "It's only been my dad and I growing up, and he died in the military. I don't have anyone to advocate for me, so I got an idea to show my skills. Yeah, I rigged the painting … *BUT* I didn't mean for you to get hurt or anything. I promise. I'm sorry you sprained your ankle." He hangs his head, no longer the cocky teen I first met. I remember the military lighter he uses, so I cut him some slack.

"Okay, apology accepted. What's second?" I cross my arms and lean against the wall.

"Second?"

"Yeah, you said at first…"

"Oh, well." He looks down the hallway cracking his neck. "I kinda wanted to photograph you. You're beautiful."

"Me?" I feel my cheeks heat up.

"Yeah, but I know now that's the impossible cause that Marco guy would never allow it." His face twists up.

"Marco doesn't have a say in what I do." I put my hands on my hips again, silently chastising myself. *When did I become so mature compared to this kid?*

He leans against the wall. "Really? Cause the guy won't leave you alone for a minute. It's as if he's attached at the hip to you. He even carried you everywhere for weeks."

"What are the photographs for?" I lower my tone.

"There's a gallery I work for doing odd jobs and helping out to make extra money. The owner says to bring him some of my work to display. I haven't found a subject worthy of a show until I saw you." Now he looks me in the eye, his blue irises mesmerizing.

I'm cool enough to be a model for him. Who knows, maybe I'll get discovered and not have to worry about a career choice, it will come to me? "I'm flattered, Alex. If it helps your art career, I'll do it."

On the way home, the chill in the air goes all the way down to my bones. It's drizzling like a foggy cloak over the city. Damp and depressing. I decide to stop at my brother's to see if Liz is free to talk. When I walk in, Clyde comes pitter-pattering up to greet me. His little spike collar makes me giggle inwardly.

"Hello, sweet baby." I pick him up and brace myself to see Marco. *I guess I can't turn around now.* Everyone is sitting in the family room; Clyde and I take a seat next to Liz.

"Something to drink?" Tony asks.

"I'll have wine if it's open."

Marco and I exchange looks, and I accept the wine from my brother.

"I didn't see your car outside," I say to Marco.

"Tony made me pull in the garage next to him. It was raining hard when we got here."

I salute him with my glass in answer. Then I turn to Liz at my side and let her know with my eyes that I need to talk. Having known each other since I was in high school, she got it.

"Let's let Clyde run around outside under the covered patio, get some fresh air," she says directly to me, but so all could hear.

"What's going on?" She shuts the slider behind her.

"I need advice." I put Clyde down to sniff around.

"Okay, shoot."

"After we talked last, I was determined to let Marco know that I wanted to be with him." She smiles, and her eyes go wide. "I jumped him after the Halloween party, and we fooled around a little."

"Was he the one? Did you guys…" She leans forward in her chair.

"No, it didn't go that far. But the way he… uh… you know…was like nothing else I've ever experienced." I can feel my face heat.

"That's good! Right?" She puts her hand over mine.

"It was… and I was so happy. But… a girl came to the mansion today looking for him. She's his girlfriend." I look down, feeling my eyes start to water.

"Oh honey, what did she look like? He already broke up with the last one."

"Her name was Caitlin… and…"

"That's her! Honey, she's just trying a hail Mary to get him back." Liz's voice rises.

"Marco and I made a deal to keep us a secret until we felt comfortable telling Tony and my parents. Do you think he wanted to leave a window open for her to come back to him?"

"No, no, not at all. Listen, when we would go out together, Marco was only going through the motions. The look on his face when he heard you come in tonight was priceless. I knew him in high school, and have gotten to know him even better since me and your brother are together again. That man has it bad for you." She hugs me.

"I'm so confused as to what to do. The one design school I've heard from is in Arizona. I'm not sure I'll get into the schools here. What happens to our relationship if I have to leave?" I back up and look her in the eyes. "Maybe I should just slow things down even though he's all I can think about."

"You'll work things out to accommodate what is best for both of you. Try not to worry. This is meant to be." She hugs me.

Clyde gets up in his hind legs for me to pick him up. "Looks like his dog has it bad too." We both laugh.

Twenty-Three

MARCO

"How about I order some pizza," Liz announces when they return.

"Sounds good! Tony follows his girl into the kitchen to stipulate the toppings."

Mimi stands in front of me with a beer offered. "Hey."

"Hey, Meems." I take the bottle and twist off the cap.

She takes a sip of wine and licks her lips, so supple and plump, waiting for a kiss. The fact I might drool is a real possibility if I don't look away.

"We should talk." I clear my throat. "Can you come to my place after the pizza?"

"Sure." She gives me a closed-mouth smile. I don't think she realizes the real reason I asked her over. I hate disappointing her.

A few hours later, no sooner than I close the door to my place, she jumps me. Clyde is hopping up, barking like crazy. Obviously, she misunderstood my wanting to talk. Her hands are unbuttoning my shirt while our lips devour each other.

"Wait…" *kiss* "I wanted…" *kiss*.

She jumps up and squeezes my waist between her thighs.

I'm so weak.

I'm going to hell.

Girls climb me like a tree because I'm so tall. Mimi's no different. It's never turned me on as much as this time. My calves hit the edge of the sofa, and I sit with her on my lap. I take her face in my hands to still the motions and get some space. Clyde jumps in between us, licking Mimi's chin.

"What's wrong?" Her face crinkles up.

Here's the moment of truth. God help me, I'm not strong enough to let her go, so I take a different tactic. "I have a question, and I want you to be honest with me." She nods within my hands. "Are you still a virgin?" Her eyes scan the ceiling, and her cheeks turn crimson. She cradles Clyde in her arms, still straddling me. The lucky guy settles in with his head on her chest.

"Marco…" she whines. "Does it really matter?"

"Yes, it matters to me."

Her eyes jump from my left eye to my right, judging my sincerity and deciding her answer.

"Yes." She puts her fingers over my lips to keep me from answering. "But, who better? To give my first time to, than a man who's cared about me since I was born?"

My hand covers hers, and I kiss the inside of her palm. "You're right." She straightens and smiles ear to ear. "But that doesn't mean we're ready for that now. I care *so much* that I want your first time to be with someone you love. Someday in the future, you may or may not feel that way about me. It may seem like a great idea with all this heat going on between us, but I have to be the practical one."

"The curse of being with an older guy is… he has too much common sense for his own good," She sighs.

"Believe me. This is **not** easy for me either. Let's enjoy each other's company and get to know each other again. I want to explore what makes Amelia happy. Talk to me." *Well, the guys would tell me I just lost my "man card" with that sentence.*

She adjusts on my lap, stretching out her legs and placing her head against my chest. Clyde is readjusting his turf until he's snuggled in on her lap. My fingers slowly comb through the silky strands of her hair.

"Let's see, what makes me happy?" I nod and kiss the top of her head. "Working with you makes me happy. Clyde makes me happy." Her fingers scratch him behind his ears.

I smile. "Clyde makes me happy too."

"My family makes me happy. The loving way my mom and dad still cherish each other. I want that long-term, be-all, end-all, love. My mom describes it as the person you wake up thinking about and go to bed doing the same. To be with that one person who has me on their mind all day too. The prospect of that kind of love still existing makes me happy."

"Your mom and dad are an inspiration to us all." I kiss the top of her head.

"Being here in your arms is happiness." She picks up Clyde and speaks to him. "Right, Clyde? Your daddy is the best!" Clyde gets excited that the attention is on him and jumps down to find a toy for her to throw at him. He disappears into my bedroom.

"What we did the last time we were alone together, pure joy." Her voice is low, almost a whisper.

"Pure joy for sure," I moan.

Her beautiful eyes and mischievous smile pop up toward me. "Pure joy now!" She slides down to the floor between my legs and places her hands on my thighs, moving upward to my zipper. She rocks my world.

Twenty-Four

AMELIA

THE *How to Give a Blow Job* articles online have paid off. Don't get me wrong, I've done it twice before in college but messed it up. I never thought it could be as sexy as it was with Marco. Since he's taken actual intercourse off the table, for now, it kinda makes me less stressed. I've been the one to instigate anything we've done because I know Marco so well and trust him. When Liz told me that he never was really into Caitlin, I knew her coming to see him was all one-sided. She hasn't been back as far as I know.

It's Thanksgiving week, and my mom is cooking up a storm getting ready. We're making pies today. As I shuffle into the house after work, she's already making the dough for the crusts.

"Hi, honey, how was work?" The rolling pin flattens out a perfect circle.

"We're off the rest of the week." I hang up my coat and join her.

"That's great! You can help me make the meatballs and gravy on Wednesday. I left a message on Marco's phone letting him know what time dinner is too."

"Oh…um… Marco's coming to Thanksgiving?" I try my best not to show I already know by washing my hands with my eyes averted.

My mom stops what she's doing and looks up at me. Her eyes filled with sparkle. "I knew it! I knew it!"

"What? Clue me in," I ask, drying each finger.

"You have feelings for Marco!" She runs over to me and throws her arms around my shoulders in a stifling hug, "Oh, sweetie, I'm so happy." She looks me in the eye, "Does he know?"

"How did you come up with that conclusion?" I twist up my face trying not to smile.

"I'm your mother." She uses her index finger under my chin to make me look at her. "I know you like the back of my right hand."

When she looks me in the eye up close, I can never lie to her, and she knows it. "Okay, Okay. Yes, I do." I plop into one of the kitchen chairs, "we've been dating, but he's not ready to tell Tony or Dad. It might all be for nothing anyway since the only design school that accepted me so far is in Arizona. We can't have a long-distance relationship. It never works even for just eight months."

"You still have time for the other schools to accept. We'll just keep our fingers crossed." She kisses me on the cheek.

The men are all so into the football games and the food on Thanksgiving that any worry about them finding out about Marco and I are unfounded. I know for sure when Daniel approaches him with a request.

"Hey, bro, you busy Friday night? I gotta girl who wants me to bring a buddy for her friend." He pretends to punch his shoulder.

Marco looks down and switches his weight from one foot to the other. "I have plans that night." He rubs his chin with his thumb and forefinger.

"Come on, man. I can't have Dominic come. It's like I'm lookin' in the fuckin' mirror all night. He distracts me." Daniel sits in the recliner and pushes backward.

"What are you afraid you'll be the insipid twin brother for once, and I'll be the center of attention," Dominic chimes in.

"Hasn't happened yet! Why worry?" Dom throws a Cheeto at Daniel. "Come on, Marco! You haven't dated since Caitlin."

"How do you know?" Marco pushes Daniel in the back of the head.

"Cause, you've been fuckin nervous as hell, like you haven't been laid since."

"Can you please stop discussing my sex life! I'm busy, and that is the fuckin end of it."

He exits into the kitchen, and I follow. "So, is it a problem?" I whisper.

"Is what a problem?" The crease between his brows deepens.

"That you haven't been laid? Or have you, and just not with me?" My hands go to my hips.

"Can we talk about this later more privately? Please."

I nod and kiss him on the cheek.

After dinner, Marco secretly follows me into the garage, where we have the extra frig.

"Oh, my goodness, you scared me. I almost dropped the limoncello." My grip on the frosted bottle tightens.

"Why didn't you turn on the lights?" His hands slink around my waist.

"Because the frig has a light and I was just gonna be a second." My voice goes up on the last word as he pulls me into him.

"Maybe I can talk you into just a few more seconds here in the dark with me?" I can feel his smile against my cheek.

"Keep rubbing that perfect body against me, and you can talk me into just about anything."

He bends, I feel his breath on my lips and the softness of his kiss. I set the bottle down on a table next to me and rise on my tiptoes to take it deeper. He tastes like heaven. The warmth of his body shields me against the dampness of the garage in the Chicago winter. I run my fingers through the hair that curls at his nape. His fingers squeeze me tighter yet.

"Mimi?" He whispers in my ear. "Did you really think that I'm seeing other girls while I'm with you?"

"Nah, not really." I pull back and face him. "I've known you all my life and trust you from head to toe." I lower my voice. "But I do worry since you put the halt on... you know... fucking, that you will lose interest in me." I can feel my cheeks heat.

"That will never happen, little one." He kisses my forehead and then searches my eyes. "You're all I think about. And, when we finally are together like that, it will be entirely different than with anyone else. I want to keep you safe and make you happy." He devours my mouth with his, and we can't get close enough... until the door opens.

We jump apart like two teenagers getting caught. The whites of Marco's eyeballs show in the light shining in from behind my mother. I shake my head and give him a don't worry look. Then I pick up the bottle and turn around to hand it to my mom. She quickly closes the door and leaves us alone.

"Great. I guess I have to talk to Tony tonight."

"No, you don't. Not if you're not ready. My mom knows. She figured it out on her own. She knows both of us like a book." I shrug.

He leans against the car and runs his fingers through his hair. The more messed up it gets, the hotter he looks.

"It's just. I'm struggling with how I would feel if I were your big brother. I have protective feelings over you like a big brother too. But now, it's morphed into this other insatiable feeling that keeps outweighing the logical protective ones."

"Marco, what are you logically protecting me from? Why do you think Tony and my dad would want to protect me from you?" I rest against him with my head on his chest.

"Baby, no guy is ever good enough for a sister or a daughter. Every man feels that way. But in this case, your brother knows how fucked up my family's been at times in my life, and he won't want you dealing with that baggage." He shifts, crossing his legs at the ankle. His fingers mindlessly comb through my hair when I come up with an idea.

"How about you talk to *me* about it. That way, I can decide for myself. Let's think about having this conversation in the near future." He shakes his head. "When you're ready."

I feel so bad that we can't continue to open up to each other. But, in my garage on Thanksgiving is not the time or place. I'd like to be honest and tell him I know about his baby sister, Julia, but I'm not sure how he'd take it. I'll have to think about it.

Twenty-Five

VINCENT DRAGONETTI ~YEAR: 1997

"I WOULD LIKE to extend my deepest condolences for the loss of your infant granddaughter, Don Fiori." I extend my hand, and he takes it. My sweaty palms, revealing my unease at being called to this meeting with the head of one of the most prominent families in the Chicago Outfit, aka 'The Chicago Mob'. I make sure to call him 'Don' since he's old school and prefers it. These days the younger heads of the families are referred to as 'boss'.

"Thank you, Vincent." He gestures for me to sit and puffs on a cigar. "I wanted to speak to you about my grandson Marco. His mother tells me his best friend is your son Anthony, and he spends many hours at your home. Even sharing meals with your family almost every day."

I nod my head. "Yes, sir."

"How many children do you have?" He lifts his head and blows the smoke upward.

"My oldest is Anthony, twin boys Daniel and Dominic, and recently blessed with an infant girl Amelia."

"The doctor told my son and daughter-in-law that your influence has been positive for Marco in his recovery of the trauma he sustained with the death of his sister, Julia."

"Anthony loves Marco like a brother. They are close, and we care very much for your grandson and his wellbeing."

"I would like to propose that you and your wife do me a favor and watch over my grandson from now on. Become his stable environment during this time when his parents are failing to do so. It is most important to me that my grandson thrives despite his birthright. If you agree, I will be indebted to you."

I wipe my hands inconspicuously on my pants. "Of course, I agree, sir. We will love and care for Marco as our own. You never have to worry that he will be alone."

Don Fiori gets up and gazes out the window. "He is a child now and won't understand such things as keeping him safe. But I have faith that as he grows into a man as honest and upstanding as you, he will understand the truth."

"Yes, sir. Thank you."

"This conversation stays between us until the day I am gone. At that time, it will be written in my will what my intentions are regarding Marco. I want him to have love and a family with a normal life outside of the family business." He turns and offers his hand to shake.

I rise to accept. "I will do my best to always be there for Marco."

"That is all I can ask. Now go, be with your family. Thank you, Vincenzo."

Twenty-Six

MARCO FIORI

TONY and his dad are in the office arguing when I return from the garage. I knock on the door. "Hey, guys, what's goin' on? Can I help?" They both turn and look at me. Then Vincent sidles around me to close the door. He exhales forcefully.

"You might be the solution to all our problems. But I need you to sit down and listen to the whole story before you get the wrong idea." I sit and nod. "Promise?"

"Yup." I give him thumbs up, not realizing the serious nature of the impending conversation.

Vince sits on the edge of his desk directly in front of me. "Have you ever wondered why your father never recruited you into the family business? You know the extent of who your grandfather controls in La Cosa Nostra, right?"

Shit, Vince is finally bringing up the topic I wanted to remain a secret. My mouth hangs open a little.

"Dad, what are you talking about?" Tony gets up, holding his arms out. I wave him off to sit back down.

"I know some of it, yeah. But I choose to remain uninvolved. I run a legitimate business, Vince."

Vincent stands. "I know, I know. That's not what this is about." He sits in his chair and leans his forearms on his desk. "When you guys were kids, you were inseparable. Still are. Mom and I loved all of you the same. Right?" Tony and I nod. "When you guys were seven, and Marco's family went through that rough time we never speak of, Don Fiori called me in for a meeting. Marco's grandfather." Vincent exhales sharply and looks directly at Tony. "Long story short, he asked me for a favor to watch over Marco as if he was my own son. I told him I already thought of him as such, and I would be happy to do so." The last words come out more quickly as if he needs to get them in.

I run my fingers through my hair. "Wait, you mean he forced you to take me into your family?" *My grandfather forced them to take me into their home?*

"NO!" He puts both hands up, palms facing me. "NO way, Marco, we already loved you as our son, I promise you. Your grandfather was asking me to do something I was already doing, son." He comes from around the desk and puts his hand on my shoulder. "Do you understand and believe me? I have no reason to lie to you. You know how much we *all* love you. You can feel it. I know you can."

Tony moves to the edge of his chair closer to us. "It's true bro, we all are your family." His eyebrows scrunch together.

"Why did my grandfather do this?" I look up at Vince.

"He never wants you to be involved in the family business. He said, and I quote, "I want Marco to be loved and have a family with a normal life. He will never take over the family business.""

I shake my head. "Guess I lucked out." I stand up and walk to the window. "What is your current problem?" I turn toward both of them. "And, how am I the answer?"

"Another rival family of your grandfather, the Ricci family, is threatening Dragon Entertainment with a ransomware virus if we don't pay them extortion money," Tony says. "I had no idea you were in *the* Fiori family."

"Dragon can't afford the ransom? Or you don't want to start something that may continue? I get it," I say.

Vince nods. "Don Fiori told me he would be indebted if I did what he asked. So maybe I ask for his help now?" Vincent's hands are on his hips, looking back and forth at us both.

"He's my grandfather, I'll ask." I start to walk to the door, but Vince stops me.

"No, you cannot because the conversation I had with him was never supposed to leave that room. I have to ask him myself."

Twenty-Seven

AMELIA DRAGONETTI

THE STUDIO ALEX has set up in his friend's home is state of the art. The friend has wealthy parents and trusts him to use the equipment.

"Make yourself comfortable. I arranged a basic set for the first few shots, and we'll move stuff around as we go." Alex scratches his head.

I remove my coat and smooth my hand over my skirt. I had no idea what to wear or to expect from the photoshoot. Finally, I decided on a black, slim skirt and a chartreuse silk blouse that ties in the front. I figured we'd wing it and see what we get.

"Maybe sit first to be more comfortable." He adjusts some of the lights.

I sit on the white chaise against a white backdrop and cross my legs. Alex starts shooting and giving me directions. He asks me to do a few standing and then to take off my boots and socks.

"I knew you'd have the prettiest little feet," he says while spreading out a fluffy fur rug across the floor. "Now, on your stomach across the rug. Rest your chin on your palm and cross your ankles in the air behind you. Good." He gets shots from all angles, moving swiftly around the set. He adjusts the way my hair falls over my shoulder, then unties the bow on my blouse, letting the tails fall haphazardly. After he takes a few shots, I get ambitious and start to pose myself.

First on my back, resting upon my elbows with a sexy backward look. "How's this?" I'm feeling like a model in a magazine shoot. Adrenaline flows through me as I change positions.

Alex lowers the camera, his blue eyes darker, expression softer. "Great. Unbutton your blouse. Fluff your hair behind you."

"Like this?" I do as he says, hearing the camera snap while my hands are running through my hair.

"Excellent! You're so beautiful. I like the edginess."

"I have another idea." I grab a dining chair and straddle it, my skirt sliding up to my upper thigh. One elbow rests on the back, supporting my head and flipping my hair to one side with a sultry look. I admit I get into being his muse, and we take some sexier shots after that. The effect on Alex is evident.

"Shit. Amazing. These will be in the gallery for sure."

"You really think so? It was fun." I'm thirsty, and down a bottle of water he gives me.

"So, what's the story between you and the hulk? He your boyfriend or your stalker?" He's looking down, adjusting buttons on the camera.

I plop into the chair, exhaling sharply. "It's complicated. But, he's not my stalker."

"Don't suppose you'd give me a chance?" He looks away and rubs his lips together. I know how hard it was to ask me that. The way he looks on the outside is insignificant when there's still just a seventeen-year-old inside. It's so funny how age has a different meaning during the phases of our lives. *Why does it feel right to be with Marco, who is twenty-nine, when I'm twenty-two next week? But Alex feels too young for me.*

He walks over to where I'm sitting and leans over the arm of the chaise. Our faces are so close I can feel his breath.

"Alex, this feels more like friends to me. I'm sorry." I put my hand over his and squeeze. "But I do have a girl I'd like you to meet that is around your age."

"Wow, shit, not only did you just put me in the friend zone, but you suggested I can't get my own woman. I'm not a fuckin loser Mimi." He gets up and starts wrapping up a cord.

"I never said you were a loser or that you can't get your own dates. I know a great girl who you might like. I promise if you say no, I won't push it. Just think about it and let me know."

"Yeah, okay." His grimace is evident before he catches himself and hides it with snarky confidence.

"Hey, I forgot to tell you that I talked to my brother at Thanksgiving, and he said to have you come to the office next week to meet him. You'll probably start with an internship, but once you show him what you know, he'll love it." I smile.

All the pretense in his attitude evaporates. He lifts me off the ground and twirls us around. "Fuck! Yeah! Thank you."

Twenty-Eight

MARCO FIORI

AMELIA'S BIRTHDAY IS FRIDAY, and I always get her a present. But this year I want to get her something special. The problem is I don't want it to show that we're together. After the conversation with Tony and his dad the other day, I feel unworthy of Amelia now more than ever. Who wants a son-in-law with blood ties to the mob? Don't get me wrong, *I* knew it before the other day. But not aware of the extent that *they* knew.

The lights in the glass cases in Tiffany are warm against my palms. I decide on a white gold link bracelet lined with miniature diamonds. It's understated, expensive, and trendy. Her birthday is near Christmas, and I don't want to think that far ahead right now, though. So, I have it wrapped and head back to the mansion.

The workmen are on the lower level, and Kimber is in her office. Amelia is nowhere around.

"Hey Kim, where's Amelia?"

"Oh, she went to her photoshoot with Alex Greyson." She cracks her gum.

"What photoshoot? Who's Alex Greyson?" I put my palms on the desk.

Kimber's brows rise, and she stops typing. "Um…uh…I think for his gallery showing. He's… I don't know who he is." She shrugs with her hands.

I back out of her office and slam the door. Why was I not told about this?" What kind of fucked up stuff is this guy talking her into?

There's work piled on my desk, and my computer is pinging from emails but, I can't concentrate on anything but what Mimi is doing. God knows she's so independent she thinks she can handle any situation. What if this guy asks her to take off her clothes? I'll fucking kill him before he displays naked pictures of her publicly. I pick up Clyde's squeaky toy and whip it against the wall.

"What did squeaky ever do to you?"

When I turn, the sight of her makes me weak she's so beautiful. It catches me off guard. The sexy administrative assistants in the movies have nothing on her. Slim skirt, fuck me heels, silky top untied, showing just a peek of her lacy bra. Red, full lips, eyes that glow accentuated with long lashes. Her hair is just the same as the Halloween party in long loose curls.

"Wow, you look amazing. Did I forget a date or something?" The reason I was angry falls away like the tide retreating into the sea.

She sways into the office and closes the door locking it behind her. Pushing me backward into my chair, she hops up on my desk and crosses her legs suggestively. "You like Mr. Fiori?" The tightness in my pants suggests I like it very much.

I run my hands up her bare legs to her thighs as she uncrosses them. Her panties are already soaked as I push them aside. A moan escapes, she unbuttons her blouse, and her perky nipples poke through the lace. I reach down and bite them right through the fabric. Her head falls backward while supporting herself with her arms. She decides quickly to take things deeper when she kicks off her shoes, pulls the skirt up to her waist, and places her bare feet on the desk opening herself fully to my perusal. Fuck, if it's not the most erotic thing I've ever seen. The main purpose in my life is to make her orgasm with my fingers and my mouth right here on my desk. By the time I'm finished, she can't walk or talk, so I pick her up and carry her to the sofa. She's cradled in my lap with her head on my shoulder, spent. I'm content holding her, just knowing she's mine. *How could I ever thought that I could fight these feelings I have for her?*

Twenty-Nine

VINCENT DRAGONETTI

THE GUARD at the gate announces my arrival. I can hardly see the drive ten feet in front of the car. "Follow me up to the house. I will guide you through the fog."

The red taillights are all I can see moving slowly down the winding drive. He turns abruptly, and an imposing stone residence rises out of the fluffy white abyss. Double entry doors with wrought iron inserts set the tone of the entrance.

Another suited bodyguard takes me from there to an office where the man himself reclines in a burgundy leather chair behind a sturdy walnut desk. The inlay matches the leather on the chair.

"Please come in, Vincenzo. What can I do for you today? I trust my grandson is well?" The twenty-two years since our last meeting has aged him considerably. A bald head and bushy grey eyebrows. His voice is weaker, more congested.

"Thank you, Don Fiori. Yes, Marco is fine." I don't offer a handshake because he stays seated.

He gestures toward the chairs. "Please sit. My debt to you is due. I assume you've come to collect on the favor I exchanged with you taking care of my grandson?"

"Yes, I need to ask for help with a recent threat to my company from the Ricci family."

"Ah, Pietro Ricci and I went to school together. What have they threatened? Maybe I can have a conversation with him and see if he can reign in his son." He takes notes down on a pad. "Alberto is head-strong, and cocky to say the least.

"They threatened with a ransomware virus shutting down Dragon Enterprises computer systems worldwide. I don't need to explain how that would affect my business."

"Of course. I get it." He leans forward, steepling his crooked fingers. "Sometimes, the younger generation lets all this stuff go to their head. Pietro and his son disagree on many things, as my son and I do. Marco's father is not of the same belief that he should remain distanced from the business. Even though Marco and his father are relatively estranged, I worry that he will ignore my last will. Since there are no other heirs, he may force Marco to succeed the head position of the family upon his death no matter my wishes."

"It pains me to hear that. Is there a way around it? There are surely trusted men in the organization that are more than willing to step up to the position. What if you specifically named one of them. Would that work?" It occurs to me fleetingly that Fiori turned the conversation to his benefit. It's almost as if he already knew what to say when I called in my marker. He's reading my reactions.

Don Fiori leans back in his chair, stroking his gray goatee.

"Don't worry yourself about my problems, Vincenzo. I promise I will take care of everything before I'm gone. There are many things to consider."

"Yes, and I would like to help Marco avoid any unpleasantness with his father."

"I may have a way for you to help the situation. And I will talk to Pietro for you. Expect a call from me by the weekend."

"You have my deepest gratitude."

Thirty

AMELIA DRAGONETTI

THERE'S snow falling on the lake outside the French doors in the family room. I'm sure we'll have a white Christmas. Today's my birthday, and mom's making my favorite, manicotti. The aroma of homemade gravy and meatballs wafts through the house. My three older brothers argue over the pool table in the other room until my dad gets up and challenges them all to a game for money. Marco should be here any minute. I can't wait to see him even if I have to behave myself. He still won't confess to the real reason he's hesitant to tell my dad about us. I thought today would be good, but he nixed the idea.

"Comere' Mimi. You hold the money." Dominic hands me the crisp one-hundred-dollar bills piled up on the table. I sit on the sofa to observe and secretly wait for my man.

It surprises me how much my twin brothers resemble each other. They are three and a half years older than me and three years younger than Tony. Dominic graduated from law school and started working at Pope, Manning, and Price recently. And Daniel is a friggin brain surgeon. Tony runs our family company Dragon Hotels and Entertainment Inc, with my dad. We are a close family, and Marco is already a part of us. I can't see them not accepting the fact that we're together. Somehow, my mind summoned him from thin air. His hand appears on my shoulder, a chaste kiss upon my cheek, before greeting my dad and brothers.

The game is cutthroat between the men of the family, with Dominic, the eventual winner. I hand him the money and kiss his cheek. "Nice goin' bro."

"They underestimate me every time," he says with a wink, then whispers, "just like everyone always does. But that's my secret weapon." I roll my eyes with a giggle at how his statement rings true.

During dinner, my dad is interrupted by a phone call. When he returns, his skin is pale white, and his eyes are glazed over. After I blow out the candles, I make my way over to him.

"Hey, what's wrong? You look like that phone call was serious."

"Nothing you need to worry your pretty little head about, princess." He kisses my cheek and hugs me tight.

After I open my gifts, Marco hands me his. Nestled in the box is a sparkling diamond link bracelet. He fastens it on my wrist and kisses me on the cheek. I catch a glimpse of my mom wiping a tear from her eye.

Nico and Samantha are having a walk-through of the two top floors the next day. The mansion still won't be finished for a few months, right before they celebrate their wedding reception here. The most important reveal Marco has in store is the pool and retractable dance floor. It is a feat in engineering. I'm proud of him.

I've set out coffee and pastry for everyone. Nico asked their whole group of friends to come and see the progression of the project. Tony and Liz are bringing her daughter Tess. Jennifer and Jaxson are bringing Jen's little sister, Eva. They all plan on taking the girls ice skating in Millennium Park afterward.

"These look good." Marco swipes an apple pastry and sits up on my desk. I pour him a cup of black coffee just like he likes it.

"You have apple jelly on your chin, Mr. Fiori. Just like the powdered sugar, you're a messy eater."

His eyes sparkle, and he grins, "All the better for you to lick it off again."

"So much food porn in this relationship… what is that about?" Moving in between his wide-set knees, I suck the sweetness, and my lips wander to his. He drops the pastry onto the wax paper and pulls me closer.

"Yesterday was difficult keeping my hands off you. You in my life again in this way is more than I deserve. But I'm determined to work on being worthy of this blessing."

His lips wander to my neck, sending shivers up my spine. I can feel my nipples pucker under my shirt heat pools in my lower belly. *This man is all I've ever wanted.*

Thirty-One

MARCO FIORI

It's ten minutes before everyone is to arrive, and my nerves are shot. This is not common for me with walk-throughs. But when you do jobs for close friends, it has to be perfect. I check the pool lights one more time and head upfront.

"They're here," Amelia yells from the front hall.

The sound of laughter and stomping of little feet fill the hallway as Tess runs in, with Eva following close behind. The whole group of my friends enter together, admiring the place. The confidence in my work takes hold, and my nerves subside.

"I can't believe how much brighter it is in here," Jennifer says, looking up.

"All the skylights we put in over the dancefloor/pool have really helped. And paint colors help too. Let's face it, the whole purpose of this place has taken a one hundred eighty-degree turn. So, the décor has too."

Jaxson looks around, scratching his head. "I kinda miss the old Club Beta." This was followed by his signature smirk. Everyone laughs, expecting Jax to say exactly that.

"Is everyone ready to see my unparalleled feat of engineering?"

"Yeah!" They say simultaneously. Nico rubs his hands together.

They all stand outside the decorative tile barrier around the dance-floor that signifies the 'no walking' zone while the floor disappears. In a locked room, on the other side, my hands on the controls, I proceed to open the levers revealing the blue waters of the swimming pool underneath the dance floor. No matter how many times I've seen it, the lights and reflections take my breath away. Then out of the corner of my eye, something moves quickly past me and toward the pool. No one else can see her from behind the barricade. Unaware that the floor is now retracted, Tess runs full speed falling into the deep end of the pool. My instincts take over, hurrying out of the control room. By the time I reach the pool, she's gone under at least a second time. The fact that my watch is on, my phone is in my pocket, and my shoes are still on my feet never enters my mind. Mid dive, I hear the screaming begin as everyone realizes what's happening. By the time Tony reaches us in the water, I've got her to the ladder, and I hand her out to Nico.

"Oh my God! Thank goodness you saw her in time!" Liz cries. Tess is in her lap coughing, but she'll be alright. Tony is already out of the pool and sitting next to them, consoling her.

The adrenaline leaves my bloodstream, and I don't try to stay on the surface. After allowing myself to sink, I feel the bottom beneath my shoes. Holding my breath comes easy. I've practiced since I was a boy. My clothes weigh me down, soaked through to the skin. The water above and all around me is like a cloak disguising my anguish. I open my mouth and scream. I curse. Cry for my baby sister Julia and how there was no one there to save her. Something inside me breaks the anger, injustice a pure unadulterated rage fills me up. The pool water disguises my tears as Amelia is poolside looking down at me when I surface, gulping for air.

There's a loud ringing in my ears. I sit on the deck and try to shake it off. My heart is about to beat out of my chest. All I can see is my sister Julia at the bottom of the pool like an apparition. I ring my fingers through my hair and feel a hand on my shoulder.

"Marco, I'm here. Are you alright?" Her voice is garbled beyond the ringing, and I violently shake off her touch.

She backs away, shocked.

There's no need for words.

She gets it.

Here it is, the break. I'm already hurting Mimi.

Thirty-Two

AMELIA

I GO BACK to Tony's house with the three of them to make sure Tess is alright. Marco's rage was too much to handle. He basically told me to leave him alone. To be honest, I think the incident triggered him. I've never seen him act that way before. I should give him some space. *I hope.*

"Marco was everyone's hero when he saved Tess. I thank God he saw her in time. I don't even want to think about what could have happened." Elizabeth steps down from putting Tess to bed. "You can't take your eyes off them for a second."

"How is she now?" I ask.

"She was scared but tired. Dropped off to the dream world right away. Hey, any thoughts on what happened to Marco afterward? I wanted to thank him." Liz grabs a blanket from a drawer.

We sit together on the sofa facing each other, and she puts the throw over both of our legs.

"He totally spaced. I don't know what came over him. Unless." I look down and zero in on a fuzz that I pick off the blanket.

"Unless what?"

"He doesn't know that I know, but his sister drowned as a toddler in their family pool. He found her." I say it low as if someone else can hear.

"Oh my God! That's *gotta* be it." She reaches for both my hands. "Poor guy was reliving that horrible incident from his childhood. Here, I think this deserves a drink." Liz hands me a glass of wine from the sofa table behind us.

"I'm going to give him some space. At least, I think that's the right thing to do. What do you think?" I sip.

"Well, since you're not supposed to know, it's all you can do, really. When the time is right, you should tell Marco you know. Give him some time, he will come around."

Just as Liz advised, I give Marco time. The walkthrough was a week before Christmas, and the crew finished the lower level two days before the holiday. Kimber was the only person in the office crew who was on the job during that week. When I talked to her, she said Marco never showed. He gave orders over the phone and via email.

Mom and dad returned today from Lake Geneva. I help mom put away groceries.

"Have you talked to Marco?" She asks, emptying the plastic bags onto the counter.

I shrug my shoulders. "I decided to give him time after Tess almost drowned in the pool at the mansion. He was not himself afterward. The last thing he said to me was to leave him alone."

Mom stops in her tracks. "I hope he's alright. I called twice to tell him what time Christmas dinner will be and got his voice mail both times." She sighs deeply. "I would ask your brother to check on him, but Tony's been busy at the hotel in Rome and won't return until Christmas Eve."

"Maybe I should go over, see if he's okay." I stop and look to see mom's expression. A smile appears as she grabs a clementine peeling it, and handing me half. "Good idea. Text me from there, so I don't worry." She presses her lips together.

I pop the last piece of fruit in my mouth and jump off the barstool. Then I realize I've never actually been to Marco's place. I spin in place to face her again.

"Mom, I need his address." If she thinks it's weird, I don't know where he lives she doesn't let on.

"Oh, sure, honey." She pulls it up in her phone, and two seconds later, it pings in mine.

"Thanks, Mom."

One quick look in the hall mirror to check my appearance, and I'm on my way. *I'm sure he's just sad and needs cheering up. I'll tell him I know about Julia; he'll be more comfortable confiding in me.*

Flurries hit my windshield, but not enough to really be wet for the wipers. The dirt gets smudged in arcs across the glass. The cars in the front kick up the muddy water from the pavement, and the cycle starts again. I hate the Chicago drippy weather. Either snow or not, all this in-between stuff sucks.

Marco's place is on Lake Shore Drive. The epitome of great architecture and ideas that a builder and engineer would want to live in. I pull into the underground parking and surprisingly find a space in the guest area. No need to stop at the desk mom had the apartment number conveniently labeled in her contacts. The elevator opens on the twenty-first floor, and the confirmation that I'm definitely in the right place hits me like a slap in the face. If I was unsure of the future earlier, this sealed the deal. *American Institute of Interior Design in Arizona, here I come.* I quickly hide in the corner of the elevator. My back up against the buttons, not to be seen. It feels like my heart is made of Legos, and someone just took a baseball bat to it. The doors finally close, and I slide down the wall just like the tears are on my face.

Thirty-Three

VINCENT DRAGONETTI

With my son Tony in Italy overseeing the remodel of our property in Rome, I am in the office much more these days than I like to be. Outside my window, I observe the Chicago skyline shrouded in cloud cover. The lake is icy and rough against the shore. I contemplate my plans to adjust the lineup of the people I depend on, keeping them closer to me. An international company such as ours is difficult to keep inside the family. I cannot recruit my son Daniel because a brain surgeon is of no use to our business, but Dominic is on his way to speak to me today. With the threats we've been getting, we can use an attorney we can trust.

There's a knock at the door, and my admin sticks her head inside. "You have a Mr. Fiori to see you, sir."

I know immediately it's not Marco because he would walk right in. I'm expecting a visit soon from Fiori. The phone call I got during Mimi's birthday party indicated a problem. Don Fiori might not have been successful in talking his old friend out of extortion of Dragon Enterprises. It was another threat giving me only till the weekend to pay up.

I wipe my hands on my pants and button my suit jacket.

"Come in."

"Sir, Mr. Fiori to see you."

"Thank you, Stephanie. Don Fiori, please come in and make yourself comfortable." I indicate the wingback chair next to the sofa in my office. "Can I offer you anything?" He waves his hand and shakes his head, settling in the chair. His beefy bodyguard assumes the position near the door with his hands clasped behind his back.

My son Dominic enters. He's smiling until he sees the bodyguard.

"Dad, you wanted to see me?"

Fiori nods in his direction, and the bodyguard moves to let him in. My son looks professional in his tailored suit and expensive shoes, befitting of his status as an attorney. I proudly introduce him to Don Fiori, and he is seated. I quickly update him on the matter being discussed so he can weigh in.

"Vincenzo, I'm afraid I was unable to bring my friend Pietro Ricci over to my way of thinking." He rubs his wrinkled hands together. "But, do not lose hope because there is a way to solve all our problems. It will just take some cooperation from you."

Dominic looks over at me with his eyes narrowed that I avoid in front of Fiori. I want him to see me as his friend.

"What will you need from me?" I use the back of my hand to wipe the sweat off my top lip.

"I will explain, my son, you see the Ricci family and the Fiori Family have an understanding under the council," Fiori says.

Dominic presses his lips together and sits up in his chair as if he knows what's coming.

Fiori continues,

"If you accept my help and investment in your company, Pietro will have no choice but to leave it alone. The mere fact that the Fiori name becomes affiliated with Dragonetti Enterprises renders it off-limits."

Dominic stands. "With due respect Don Fiori, how do we know the council didn't just dream all this up to gain control of our successful company? Maybe we need to talk to the FBI?"

The bodyguard steps forward two steps. I give Dominic a look to calm down.

"I assure you that many before you have gone the same route as you describe. In the end, only to still lose the entire company. The council will always prevail." He raises his palm facing us. "Please sit, Dominic. I want you to understand my position in this matter. I want to help your father keep his company because he has done me a personal favor in the past. I trust him and will one day call on him again for another favor. So, you see, I have his best interest as my top priority." Fiori uses his hands when he talks.

"What do you propose are the details of the merger?" I glance at my son again to subliminally tell him only to listen. But I am proud of his courage in challenging Fiori. I didn't get to explain how to handle the Don before he arrived.

"I will be forty-nine percent owner leaving you with the majority fifty-one percent. The name will remain the same, and I will be a silent partner to the public. For all other purposes, to keep the company protected, I will be an owner as far as the family's council is concerned."

"The extortionist only gave me till the weekend to pay. Will it work?" I ask.

"With all due respect Don Fiori, I'm not sure it is in the company's best interest to mingle its assets with yours," Dominic interjects.

"As I said, *Vincenzo*, the public will be none the wiser. I already own hotels, and this would fall under the same part of my holdings. You really have no choice. If the Ricci family continues to harass you, it will end up with Alberto and Pietro Ricci owning your whole company. That is their objective."

Dominic is ready to pounce as soon as I come back to my office after walking them out.

"What the hell is going on? Since when do you do favors for the mafia? And why are you giving in to extortion?" Dominic is just as expressive with his hands now.

I sit behind my desk and gesture for my son to sit too. "I'm not giving in to it. He's helping us out of it. It's a long story, but he asked me to watch over Marco and raise him around the time Mimi was born. Marco's sister died in an accident, and the family fell apart. We had already brought him into the family as Anthony's best friend, so it wasn't such a difficult favor to grant to him. I had no idea it would lead to a lifelong attachment to the mob!"

"It feels that there has to be more to the story. He's keeping something from us. I don't trust him as far as I can throw him." He exhales forcefully.

"Well, because of who he is, there's no way to know until he's ready to tell us, so forget about it for now, and let's discuss why I asked you here."

"There's more?" He sits in the chair with his elbows resting on his knees.

"I want you to come work as the attorney for Dragon." He looks down at the floor. "I know you like working at Pope, Manning, and Price, but I'll pay you double."

He chuckles, sitting back and resting his ankle on his opposite knee, "I like it, but it would be great to work here with you and Tony. It was always my intention after I got some more experience under my belt. So, yes, I'll give them my resignation tomorrow and start here in two weeks."

"Excellent! I need you here with us, son. We are strong when we show a united front." I hug my son, happy to have him working by my side very soon. I feel like the more people I trust next to me, the better.

Thirty-Four

AMELIA

Christmas day is uneventful except for the frozen sleet sticking on the trees until Tony walks in with Marco by his side. Clyde jumps down and runs straight for me. He feels so good in my arms, his little tongue going crazy licking my cheek. The first consoling feeling I've felt in days. I can't even look at Marco.

It's a good thing that after dinner, the guys are all hanging in the pool room talking, and I can avoid them most of the time. My mom says I should give Marco a chance to explain, but it's too late since I've accepted my spot at the American Institute of Interior Design in Arizona. Fate stepped in and sent me there at just the time where we are estranged. I can't forgive him for being with Caitlin.

"He looks so sad." Liz sits down on my bed next to me and scratches Clyde's belly. "I think he knows your leaving."

"Well, if he wanted me to stay that much, he wouldn't be entertaining other women in his place. You should have seen him. All he had on was grey sweatpants and no shirt. He even had just fucked hair."

"What was she wearing?" She lies down with Clyde on her chest.

"She was poured into a bandeau dress with come fuck me heels. Palms on his chest, looking up into his eyes," I scoff.

Liz blows air through pierced lips. "I don't get it. The man was never that into Caitlin when they were dating."

"Well, he seems to have changed his mind," I say more forcefully than I should to Liz.

Against the wall next to my desk are the sexy pictures that Alex Grayson took of me. So, I grab them to show Liz. We spread them all over the bed and desk to pick our favorites.

"Ohh, this one is hot! Has Alex picked the ones to go up in the gallery?" She holds up the one with my blouse almost off, and my skirt hiked up, showing thigh.

"He says he has his favorites but wants my opinion. He wants my top five. Help me choose." I flip through and separate a few.

There's a knock at the door, and Liz turns to open it since she's closer. *It's him.*

"Hey, girls, my dog's been kidnapped." His eyes zero in on the photo, with my body only half-turned to the camera looking backward. My right hand is holding up my silk top just enough to cover my bare breasts. I'm leaning back on my left. Marco's facial expressions switch quickly from smiling, to lust, to anger. Elizabeth mumbles something about finding Tony and leaves, quickly closing the door.

"I wanted to say goodbye to you before you leave for Arizona on a happy note." He blows out a breath and runs his fingers through his hair. "But seeing these..." he picks up and tosses a photo onto the bed. "What were you thinking? I can't believe you took your clothes off for a photographer, Amelia!"

"It's not like there's anything showing! I think they're tasteful and sexy. Some of them will be in a gallery downtown. It's all considered art." I roll my eyes.

"What about the photographer? "He steps toward me. "I bet he had fun posing your naked body, huh?" His eyes are wild and filled with anger. The sight of him makes me just as angry.

"What about you with Caitlin hanging all over your half-naked body? Touching you." I hold up my hands and wiggle my fingers to be more sardonic.

He's taken aback, his eyebrows scrunched together. Since it seems like minutes of him trying to place what I'm talking about, I fill him in myself. "I was at your apartment the other day to check on you, and *she* was there, *stuck* to your naked torso like glue. By the way, those grey sweatpants leave nothing to the imagination. From where I was standing, I could see the whole outline of your junk before she attacked you. The evidence conclusive you liked it." I turn, unable to look at him anymore. *I can't let him see how much it hurts.*

I feel him closer behind me. He reaches out and gently pulls me back to face him. His expression softens along with his tone of voice. "What you saw was me throwing Caitlin out of my apartment. She snuck in and crawled into my bed with me. The sweatpants were what I had on the floor to put on quickly. She woke me up, so my *junk* was more noticeable because it was morning. Caitlin hasn't been the source of my arousal for a very long time." His eyes travel down my body.

"Oh yeah, and you just let her slobber all over you in the doorway while you're throwing her out? I'm supposed to believe all this bull-shit?" I tug out of his grasp.

There's hurt replacing all the anger in his tone. "Amelia, please, you have to believe me. I don't know how much you saw, but I took away her keys to my apartment so she couldn't get in anymore on a whim. Then I made sure she understood that it's over between the two of us. You have to believe me, Little One." The look in his eyes is incomparable. The sadness that has taken up residence there is real.

"Why do you even care what I think?" All I can think of is Caitlin standing at his door with her arms around his neck, her legs locked around his waist. I turn my back to him so the tears that threaten to surface will go unnoticed. "The fact that you let her climb you like a tree... and... and..."

"That means nothing! *I'm tall*, girls that want in my face climb me like a tree! You've even done it yourself. I put her down just as fast as she climbed up. Did you see it?"

I shake my head, gazing out my window. He's over to me again in two strides, strong arms around me, my back to his front. Marco moves my hair and whispers in my ear. "It makes me crazy thinking about you naked in front of any other man. I could kill him with my bare hands."

"He didn't see anything. I was discreet in how I disrobed." I don't fight him because it feels so good to be in his arms, even if we're arguing.

"No other woman ever made me feel the way you did when you climbed me like a tree. Our souls speak to each other." I can feel him smile, and I allow myself to lean back a little. "It's in my bone marrow Meems. It's in my blood pumping through my godforsaken heart to care for and protect you. It's all that's important to me, even over my wants or needs."

Thirty-Five

MARCO

It feels good to hold her in my arms again after the agonizing week I've had. Letting myself have these few minutes of sweetness is selfish. I'm just going to turn around and let her go. But I can't help it. I'm only human. Without Mimi near me, It will be impossible to breathe. My world will go dark.

"I wish I knew that before I made the final decision to leave." She relaxes in my arms.

"Leaving is the best thing for you to do. You made the right decision." I take a whiff of her coconut and lavender scent, feel the silkiness of her hair, and burn it into my brain cause as soon as she turns to look at me, I have to break both of our hearts.

She whips around, eyes wide. "You don't realize how powerful words are. How can you tell me in one breath that I'm all that matters to you and in the next that I should leave you for a year?" Her arms fold across her chest, locking me out. *I don't blame her.*

Using my thumb and forefinger to rub my eyes, I take a second. "I'm not the best thing for you right now. Making your dreams come true of a career in design should come first. I care so much for you that

I need to protect you from *me*." He clears his throat. "From missing out on a great opportunity just to stay here with *me*."

"What about what I want!" All you've done is treat me like a child. I'm not your little sister! You couldn't save her, and it's not your job to save me!" Her hand covers her mouth like she's just as surprised at what came out of it as I am.

Blink.

I close my eyes, and my head falls back at the power of that statement.

I move some pictures over and sit on the bed, my elbows resting on my knees, head in my palms. "All this time. You knew?"

"I'm sorry... so sorry, Marco. I didn't mean to say..."

"It's okay... I'm fucked up because of it. You should stay away from me." I rise and pick up Clyde. *Does everyone know that if I came home from school on time, I would have been able to save my little sister? Did my parents or my grandfather tell them? Does she know about my mother too?* One last look at her before I close the door. Tears are streaming silently down her face. "Go and be happy."

The next few days, I hibernate in my condo with Clyde. My sweatpants become my uniform, and delivered pizza is the staple meal. The urge to check on Mimi is overwhelming. Scenarios of her meeting someone else and never returning home to Chicago fill my mind. *What if she loves it there and wants to stay? The school could place her in a design job, and she could stay. I may have fucked up my chances for good.*

The American Institute of Interior Design website says the program is twenty-seven weeks. I cross my fingers that she can take the quickest route. Our chances are better the sooner she finishes. My mind goes quickly from hope to despair and back again. To a point where I think I'm going crazy. Since I purposely give my crew some time off, I decide to see a therapist and get my head straight. Twice a week in the next several weeks.

Every day I wake to want to hear her voice, see her beautiful face and smell her scent. Mimi is my hope, my happiness, even if I need to give her up. After a couple of weeks of seeing the therapist, doing the exercises, and reading the books, I start to feel better. I've never actually voiced my guilt and sorrow out loud. Doing that is cathartic, especially to someone who knows how to interpret it. She explains and makes me think about how we have no control over many things in our lives. There are ways to cope. To deal with the blame recognition and let it go for the good of your sanity. She told me to think about it differently. In a way, the time I spent screaming under the surface of the pool washed me clean. Saving Tess was a sort of rebirth that numbed my guilt and brought forth something I'd been missing but needed so badly. Forgiveness.

Clyde licks my grandmother's cheek, and she giggles. The care facility Nana is in seems nice. They mop the floors, wipe down the doors and handles along with the wheelchairs daily. My grandmother's room is peach and light green, just like her home was when I was little.

"How are you feeling Nana?" I sit in the chair next to her bed.

"I'm so happy to see my babies." She hugs the puppy closer playing with his big ears.

Nana refers to Clyde and me as her babies. Ever since my mom passed away, Nana and I have stayed close. My father remarried Marcella, a girl only about twelve years older than me. I drifted apart from his new family when they had a daughter, Vanessa. Dad seemed only interested in his new family. I was lucky to have Nana and the Dragonettis'. Nana still blames my father for her daughter dying so young. She tells the story almost every time I come here.

"Your mother was a beautiful girl. In high school, she had two boys fighting over her all four years. I truly believed she was in love with both boys and chose one after being forced to." My grandmother gets a faraway look in her eyes. "The boy she should have married was caring and protective. He was soft-spoken and so handsome, just like you." She lifts my hand in hers and kisses the back of it. "Gianmarco was loud and demanding. He gave orders, not requests. If only Mia could disobey your controlling grandfather, she would still be here. Victor insisted she go out with Gino and forbade her from seeing the other boy. That monster, Gino, didn't even let me say goodbye to my daughter. He had her cremated immediately." Nana wipes a tear.

"I know, Nana, that's all in the past now. Gino is married to Marcella now, and mom is in heaven." I pat her hand.

"You don't know, sweetheart. Gino is the devil. He killed your mother! When Don Fiori dies, he will become boss, and I fear for your life. I need to tell you now because I'm old, and I may forget." She sits up in bed, agitated, and the nurse rushes in. "Mia comes to see me sometimes. Does she visit you?" Her eyes fill with tears.

"No, Nana. I'm sorry I upset you."

The nurse calms my grandmother down, and she falls asleep. I take Clyde, kiss her forehead and leave. Walking to my car, I contemplate that this is the first time she actually pinned my father with my mother's death. I've always been uncomfortable with the cause of death being suicide. My mom was devoted to me. I never believed she would willingly take her own life. I just thought it was a mistake, and she overdosed by accident. *Is Nana just becoming senile or really wanting to tell me the truth? My father is the next in line to become boss, so it wouldn't be hard for him to get away with murder. Is this the rambling of her decline into dementia or a warning?*

Thirty-Six

VINCENT

I drive Amelia to the airport with my wife. The fact that it's snowing and the planes all need to be deiced crosses my mind. But what's worse is knowing she's going to be alone for possibly a year in Arizona. It makes me uneasy. Girls are so much harder to raise than boys. She's my little girl, and letting go is difficult.

"Daddy, are you paying attention? The airline is right there, don't pass it up." She reaches up from the back seat, pointing.

"Sorry, honey, I was daydreaming."

We pull all her bags out and hug her almost too hard goodbye. Lucia has tears in her eyes, and I know she's thinking the same thoughts. Amelia smiles and reassures us.

"Don't worry, you two. I will call you all the time. And video chat at Sunday dinners with everyone." We hug again. Lucia wipes her eyes with a tissue.

"Okay, honey! Be careful. We love you!" We stand there waving like zombies until a horn beeps behind us.

That was a few weeks ago. Mimi seems to be doing well at school. She's settling into her apartment in Fountain Hills near her classes. I made sure the condo we rented was in a safe area with lots of restaurants and shopping.

Work has been busy, and I can truly say that having two of my sons here is the best thing to happen to this company in a long time. We also have a new intern, Alex Greyson. Amelia showed Tony some of his work, and he hired him. Alex is killing it in the gaming division of the company. It seems he'll be an asset to us. Tony can train him the right way because he's young.

Dominic investigates the companies taken over by the council. He also researches the ones who failed to cooperate and are now defunct. Don Fiori's plan is the best way to keep the majority holdings in the company and still thrive as a whole. Dominic composes the paperwork with the stipulation that if anything happens to Don Fiori, his shares refer back to the Dragonetti family, namely me. Surprisingly, he agrees, and we move forward. It's difficult to guess what's going on in someone else's mind to prepare or plan, so we sign the contracts and put out the fire that's in front of us now. Consequently, for the next few months, we have had no threatening phone calls or emails. Everything is business as usual until I'm watching the news on a Sunday evening in the den.

'Gianfranco Fiori has been admitted to Northwestern Memorial Hospital. There are rumors that his illness could be life-threatening, and an update will follow later in the news at ten.

The first thing I must do is call Marco. Even though he and Gino aren't close, I'm sure he'll go to the hospital. Once in my office, a call rings through my computer with a video chat from my daughter.

"Hi daddy, did you see the news about Marco's father?" She looks worried and a little tired.

"Yeah, sweetheart, I was just about to call him."

"Do you…"

The doorbell rings.

"Hold on, sweetie." I hear my wife introducing herself as she escorts Don Fiori and his bodyguard into my house. "I'll call you back, Amelia."

My wife stands with her back to me, gesturing to the men to enter my office. "Can I offer you anything?" She asks.

"How about coffee Lucia?" I stand to greet them.

"Coming right up, dear." She smiles at me and disappears down the hall.

The Don sits while his companion waits in the hallway. My wife enters a few seconds later with coffee and pastries on a tray, pours us each a cup, and then leaves.

"Your wife, Lucia, she's a beautiful woman. You are a lucky man Vincenzo." He brushes lint off his trousers. He never wavers. An unaffected blank expression is always on his face.

"Thank you, sir. Yes, I am. The news that your son has taken ill is unfortunate. I'm sorry."

"It is unfortunate and also the reason I am here to see you." He makes stern eye contact.

My hands feel sweaty. I can't tell what Fiori's thinking or if he's thinking at all. How did I get myself involved in this? What is the next item on this mob boss's agenda involving my family? Reading him is impossible, and it makes me nervous more than anything.

Thirty-Seven

AMELIA

My father is unaware that the call is never disconnected on his laptop. He must have just put the cover down halfway and left it. I can hear people entering his office and can't help but listen when it's apparent that the visitor is Marco's grandfather.

My father: "The news that your son has taken ill is unfortunate. I'm sorry."

Mr. Fiori: "It is unfortunate and also the reason I am here to see you."

My father: "What can I do to help?"

Mr. Fiori: "The doctors tell me my son has an inoperable brain tumor. They say only a handful of surgeons would attempt to remove it, and they are all in other countries. I don't have the luxury of time to bring them here, and Gino is too sick to be transported. I want your son Daniel the brain surgeon, to attempt to remove the tumor."

My father: "But Don Fiori... what...if..."

Mr. Fiori: "Hold on, Vincenzo. That's only my first request. Second is not as easy as the first."

There's a pause and heavy breathing before the older man continues. I put up the volume and listen carefully.

*"When I asked you long ago to take care of Marco, it was with this day in mind. It is because Marco can **never** be head of the Fiori Family. My son Gino will most likely succumb to this brain tumor, and I am old. There is no more blood offspring to take over the responsibilities of the business. It is my job to choose who will succeed in my place as head of the Fiori dynasty. We are in business together now; I respect you and your lovely Italian family. I've chosen **you** to take my place when I'm gone."*

My father: "Don Fiori, I'm flattered you would trust me with such a prestigious position. But with all due respect, why would you keep Marco from his family legacy and give it to an outsider? Will the council allow that to happen?"

Don Fiori: "The council will follow what I say because I am the eldest boss."

My father: "But, sir..."

Don Fiori: "If you must know the truth..." There's a pause in the conversation. *"Marco is not my biological grandson. His mother had an affair. He is never to be named head of the Fiori family because his blood is of a rival family."*

After that revelation, I can't wrap my head around the rest of the conversation. I will talk to my father about all of it later. *What should I do? Marco has a right to know he's lived a lie all his life. No wonder he thought of us as his family. He's so fragile right now though, I won't be the one to tell him this.*

After sitting in shock for a while, looking out at the palm trees swaying in the wind, I decide to research the Fiori family on my computer. It turns out they are the top family in the Chicago region of the outfit, aka the 'mob'. *I just witnessed my own father being chosen for the position of 'boss' in the mob? This is crazy.*

Outside the window, a wall of sand is blowing through the sky. The locals call it a haboob. They say to avoid driving and going out into the sand storms. My mind wanders to how it must hurt to walk through it, like a sandblaster on your skin. As usual, Marco pops back into my head. I feel so badly for him. It's all too much, so I pour myself a glass of wine and wait for my father to call me back and answer some questions.

Thirty-Eight

MARCO

NORTHWESTERN MEMORIAL HOSPITAL is supposed to be number one for brain-related illnesses. When it comes to getting my father the best care available, I know my grandfather will spare no expense. The smell of antiseptic assaults my nasal passages as I make my way to my father's room. Gino is sitting up with just the nasal cannula delivering oxygen. You'd never know there was anything life-threatening wrong with him.

"Good morning, son. Thank you for coming. The doctor's prognosis is not so good, and I wanted to see you at least one last time." I hug him gingerly then sit at his bedside.

"I thought they're gonna do surgery and remove the tumor?"

"Yeah, we have a surgeon who will attempt it, but my odds? Not so good, son." He shakes his head.

"Try and think more positively."

Just then, Daniel Dragonetti walks into the room with a nurse. "Hello, Mr. Fiori. Your father requested I come evaluate your eligibility for surgical removal of your tumor." He then notices me. "Hey, bro, how you holding up?" We shake hands and bro hug.

Daniel and I have virtually grown up together. I can easily say that he'd be the surgeon with the balls to pull off a miracle. My father will be in good hands.

"I'm okay, what's your take on all this?" I watch the nurse take my dad's vitals.

"I'm just taking over his case now. After all the tests are back, I'll have a better handle on our plan of attack." Daniel taps on the keyboard of an iPad.

"I like that! Plan of attack." My father perks up.

"As soon as I know anything, I'll return. If you're not here, bro, I'll call you."

"Thanks, man."

We shake hands, and he takes his iPad and leaves. My dad and I watch some television, and all the while, my grandmother's accusations run through my mind. I figure if I'm ever able to ask him, now's the time. I grab the remote and lower the sound.

"Hey Dad, when you found mom... you know um... was there any reason to think it may not have been suicide?"

"Why you bringin' up such unpleasantness, son? What makes you question the investigation?" His face contorts into a grimace.

"I don't know." I shrug. "Nana was talking about it and still has doubts that mom would take her own life."

"Don't waste your time bothering with the ramblings of a senile old lady. Everyone loved your mother. Nobody would ever purposely hurt her. They'd have to deal with my wrath." He sighs deeply. "I loved that woman more than life, and she left me. It took me a long time to come to terms with the fact that she would take her own life without giving me a second thought. But you know, son, she never recovered after your sister's death. I know you suffered too. I'm sorry, Marco." He shakes his head, looking down at the sheets. If he's lying, he's a pretty good actor.

"I know."

We're interrupted by my dad's current wife, Marcella, and his daughter, Vanessa.

"Marco, it's so good to see you. You know you don't come around often enough," Marcella says as she hugs me.

Vanessa hugs me too. Ten years younger than me, eighteen going on nineteen soon and turning into a beautiful young lady. She has the same body type as her mother, very voluptuous, which is surely what attracted my father to Marcella in the first place.

"Dad, I brought you ice cream. Your favorite flavor." She hops up on the bed next to him and offers him a spoonful. They're comfortable together as if this is an everyday thing.

I couldn't even tell you his favorite flavor if my life depended on it, but I know Vincent likes Spumoni. Guess I'm better off an adopted Dragonetti anyway. I say my goodbyes with a promise to keep in touch.

While passing through the electronic doors of the hospital to the parking lot, I button my coat against the icy wind. The sun has broken through the clouds for a minute but is not warm enough to feel it with the wind chill. A really hot girl stops in her tracks and blinks several times at me. It's as if I'm some kind of fucking ghost. It's so awkward that I sidestep around her and just say, excuse me. As soon as my ass hits the seat of my car and I close the door, she's at the window motioning for me to roll it down.

"Listen, I know this sounds real forward, but I feel like I know you from somewhere." She leans into the window, leaving nothing to my imagination as to the size of her tits. Long flaming red hair drapes down around her face as she uses her long manicured digits to tame it. *I've always wondered how girls with such long nails can pick up anything.*

"I'm sorry. I don't remember meeting you." I offer my hand. "I'm Marco Fiori."

She takes it. "Lana Riley. How about you join me for a cup of coffee so we can discuss where we might have met?" She stands straight and removes her sunglasses to reveal sparkling green eyes. I decide that today has been so strange already, might as well jump in with two feet. I haven't had lunch, so I take her to my favorite restaurant in the nearby neighborhood, Tuscany.

"Did you grow up here in the city?" She places her napkin on her lap and sips her water.

"Winnetka. How about you?"

"Evanston. It was just my mom and me. She passed away last year with Cancer."

"Sorry to hear that. So, where do you think we would have met?"

Those claws rake through her hair again as she looks up through her lashes at me. "Your last name's Fiori. I'm sure it was at some party with the good ole boys."

"I don't make it a habit of attending any parties with *the good ole boys*. Just because my name's Fiori doesn't mean I'm connected." My brow furrows.

Her eyes get round, and her forehead wrinkles. "Ooh, this sounds like it could be interesting. Tell me more." She leans forward in her chair.

"Nothing else to tell, I own a legitimate engineering and construction business." I shrug with my hands.

"How are you related to Gianmarco Fiori?"

"He's my grandfather, and Gianmarco Fiori Jr. is my father, but he goes by Gino."

She smirks and pushes her plate away, signaling she's finished, "You expect me to believe you think you're *not* connected?" She whispers the last part.

"In name only. I'm not a part of their business, and they're not a part of mine." The waiter collects both our plates and cleans any crumbs from the table. I signal for the check.

The ride back to the hospital parking for her car is quiet. When she opens her door to exit the car, she turns. "Let's exchange numbers, so if I come up with how I know you, I can call you. Or if you want some company, call me anytime."

I don't refuse to be polite, even though I know there's only one woman I wanna be with, and she's in sunny Arizona right now.

Thirty-Nine

VINCENT

THE STIFF DRINK does nothing to take the edge off my nerves after Fiori leaves my home. So, I down another scotch, compose myself, and return my daughter's phone call.

"Hi sweetheart, sorry it took so long to call you back." The video call loads so we can see each other.

Amelia's face is red, and her hair is disheveled. Looks like she's been pulling on it. "Don't give me that cool, calm, and collected act, Daddy. I heard most of your conversation with Mr. Fiori. You forgot to actually hang up and just put the lid down."

I can see my face fall and the color retreat from it in the little window up at the top right of my screen. "What did you hear Amelia? This is serious. You cannot divulge any information to anyone, or our lives could be in danger."

She frowns at me into the camera. "Start from the beginning, Daddy. How have you gotten us involved with the mob?"

"Believe me, darling, this is the last situation I wanted to find myself in at my age. It just kind of took on a life of its own. It has been out of my control from day one.

It all started when Don Fiori summoned me in 1997. He is the head of the Chicago Outfit known as the Chicago Mob. His request was for me to care for Marco as my own. Since we already were, I agreed. Marco's family was going through a rough time."

"Mom told me about his sister already." She licks her lips.

"Okay, so, fast forward to September last year. The company is threatened by some mob guys that if we refuse to cooperate, they will infect us with some cyber virus. I consulted with your brother and Marco, and we decided the best thing to do was talk to Don Fiori. He supposedly tried to get the other family to lay off the company but claimed he couldn't. Fiori then talks us into letting him buy forty-nine percent of the stock. As part-owner, the Fiori name prevents any other crime family from hammering us with extortion.

"Like he's our protection, keeping the predators away? It's like trading one kind of shakedown for another."

"Yeah. Now, the Don hits me with this zinger that he wants *me* to take over as head of the family. If something happens to him and his son Gino. I gotta tell ya, sweetie, it wasn't something I ever expected in a million years." I rub my weary eyes.

"I bet. So, all this is because Fiori never wants Marco to have the position?"

I pause a second to think if telling Mimi the secret is wise. The man and his secrets are dangerous. But she already heard it anyway. So, I repeat it again to clarify.

"He admitted that Marco is not a Fiori by blood and must never take over."

"It makes me wonder what the story is behind that? Does Marco know?" She tilts her head.

"Didn't you hear him say no one knows? You cannot tell anyone. I'm supposed to meet the council to take a vow of Omerta, meaning silence on all matters pertaining to the outfit. It kinda feels like he's been planning this all these years and implementing each step little by little. Fiori has sucked in my whole family." I shake my head and look up at the ceiling.

"I'm stuck here in Arizona with the class schedule. I wish I could be there to provide moral support for you, Daddy."

"It's okay, honey Dominic already knows. Now I need to explain to

Daniel that he has to save Gino Fiori for my sake as well as the Fiori family."

"Call me if you need anything. Good luck daddy, I love you." She blows me a kiss.

"Love you too, sweet pea."

Forty

MARCO

THINGS HAVE JUST BEEN WAY TOO weird lately. Amelia missing from my life, my dad suddenly ill, my grandmother accusing my father of killing my mother, and strange women in parking lots wanting my phone number. I find myself driving to the place that has always been my sanctuary. The place where I go for reason and wisdom. As soon as I walk in the door, it smells heavenly.

"Marco darling, I've just made some focaccia. Sit down and have some." Mama D is ready to feed me whenever I show up. I hug her and sit where I spent eating many meals as a child. As Amelia gets older, the similarities in her features to her moms are becoming more and more apparent. Lucia is a beautiful, warm, and loving person whose inner light has always made me feel loved unconditionally. That light is within Mimi and is what I'm hopelessly drawn to. Forever alienating any other woman who dared to be in my life.

The bread is light and flaky, with tomato, olive oil, and oregano bursting on my tongue. "Oh wow, this is so good. I'll have another."

She cuts another slice of warm focaccia and then sits at the table with me, drinking coffee. "How are you doing, dear? I know you've slowed down on jobs for the time being."

"I've taken some time to come to grips with my family's past.

Through therapy, I've been able to put some things behind me. I have a new perspective on Julia's death. But I still sometimes question my mother's suicide. I still can't believe she would take her own life and purposely leave us." I fold the napkin and set it on the empty plate. "My grandmother keeps insisting that she was murdered. I don't know what to think."

Lucia puts her hand on top of mine. "Sweetheart, your mother and I were friends, as you know. I was worried about her at the time because she was so depressed. Depression is a monumental thing to overcome. I read books and studied about it after it happened, and they made me somewhat understand the way your mom's mind was working. People who are so deep in depression that they cause harm to themselves are looking for a way to actually make the pain stop within themselves. They are not thinking of anyone else or anything else. Just peace inside themselves, stopping the agony. It's like when you burn yourself, you pull away from the source of the pain and seek comfort from the burning. They see death as the only cure." Her face scrunches. "On the other hand, if you still question the cause of death from the coroner, you should talk to your father about the doubt."

I inhale a big breath and exhale. "I asked Gino, and he skirted around it."

"Don't let him get away with not giving you answers. Ask him again."

"I'll try. We don't really talk, so it's hard. But, yeah, I've been taking sort of a mental health break." Changing the subject, I shift in my seat, leaning back a little. "I'm turning thirty this year. Getting my head straight on what direction I want to go with my life is a top priority."

"Have you come to any conclusions?" She folds her hands in front of her, interlocking her fingers.

"It finally feels like I'm ready to try to let go of all the heartache from my past. I've worked hard and made lots of money where that doesn't have to be my priority anymore. I want to concentrate on love and happiness in the future. I've spent too much of my life looking back, never being able to change a thing. The future is something we can change, and I intend to do that for the positive." I smile.

"Oh sweetheart, that's so wonderful!" She reaches over to hug me. "Anyone I know spending that future with you?" Her lips press together, and her eyebrows hit her hairline.

I look down at the floor. "Mimi is not happy with the fact that I told her to go to Arizona. But I thought she should follow her dream of becoming a designer. If I stood in her way, she might have resented me for it later."

"You, my darling, are wise beyond your years. Look at me, sweetie. You did the right thing even if she didn't agree with it at the time. Her time away is almost over, and it went by pretty quickly. She'll get over her unhappiness with you."

"I hope so. Clyde is even moping around without seeing her." We both laugh.

"I know you're on board with Amelia and I being together." She nods. "But I'm not so sure how Vince and the guys will take the news. Especially Tony, since I'm his best friend, he might see it as a betrayal. She's his sister and Vince's only little girl." I can hear my voice go up at the end of that last sentence showcasing my angst.

"Marco, think of how much all of them have loved you as one of our own all these years. Who better to love and take care of your most cherished, irreplaceable piece of your heart? But another piece of that heart? Someone who's just as cherished and irreplaceable." Her eyes well up, and she takes my hands inside her own. "The boys will love the fact that you will protect and love her as if it was them doing it themselves. It can't be better than that." I squeeze our conjoined hands, smiling.

"Thank you for saying that and putting my mind at rest." I exhale.

"I have an idea. Why don't you fly out and surprise Amelia? You're off work right now. She'd flip seeing you in Arizona. I can't think of a better romantic gesture."

"You're a wise woman, Mama D. I think that's just what I need right now. I'm gonna call Daniel and see when he's scheduling my father's surgery and make my reservations."

Daniel calls me back an hour later with the test results from the hospital. I put the phone on speaker so Mama D can hear his diagnosis too.

"Not every single test has returned, but I can safely say that we will not operate until some of your father's numbers come down a bit. It would be too dangerous. At least a week or ten days. Then we do all the tests again."

"Okay, Dan, thanks for keeping me in the loop."

"No problem. Hey, Mom. Save me some focaccia too."

"I will, son. Get over to see me soon."

"I will gotta go."

With that news, I make a one-way open-ended ticket to Arizona to make up with Amelia. I'll see if it will be a week or ten days, depending on my dad's surgery.

Forty-One

AMELIA

THE TEACHER IS DRONING on and on, and all I can think about is my dad and Marco. The worry is making me crazy and taking away all my concentration. Anxiety propels me straight home to my condo after class, even though many of my friends went to old town Scottsdale to party. The weather is perfect, without any humidity. Just right to make every day a good hair day. The gardenia bush next to my parking spot is especially fragrant today. That's my thought as I roll up my window, turn off my car, and look in the rearview. When I open the door and head toward the outdoor staircase, the sight has to be a mirage in this desert called Arizona.

A Fiori fantasy here in the flesh sitting on the bottom step. Seeing Marco here so close reminds me of my most recent dream. A blush singes my cheeks from a brief mental replay of the climax he delivered. Based on the incinerator behind Marco's smoky eyes, he's a mind reader. The intensity in his stare has my panties damp and my legs wobbly. When he stands, every atom inside me wants to climb him like a tree and tangle myself around him eternally.

I blink to gain some clarity, and all the details of the phone call with my father come front and center. I can't tell Marco *anything,* even though I know the secrets to the most crucial parts of his life. His expression changes must be in response to my own. So many unspoken feelings bounce like a soccer ball between us on my short walk to the stairway. *I'm so unsure as to how to even act. Should I be welcoming? Angry still? Apologetic?* I'll let him take the lead.

"Hey, little one." He opens his arms for a hug.

"Hey," I murmur into the cuts of muscle under his thin tee. His arms engulf my upper body squeezing me tight. I revel in his scent, my lower belly aching for him.

"What are you doing here?"

"I needed to see you. To explain some things, get your opinion on important matters. Cause you and me, we talk about stuff and help each other through things since we were kids. Right?" I nod, still in his embrace.

Marco's always been there for me when I needed him. Even when no one else was around to play with me when I was a little girl, he would step up. My life has been made safer and happier with him in it. I couldn't imagine growing up without him around. Now we stand at a precipice, and I know he feels it too. We're both afraid of losing what we've built over a lifetime for a romantic relationship that might not last.

"Come on up, let's talk." I let go and hop up the three flights to my condo, thinking about him ogling my ass and liking it. Once inside, he looks around while I get out some mugs for coffee. I make him one, just like he loves it, and hand it to him. I place mine on the dining table and sit.

"Nice place to spend the few months here. You like it?" He puts his cup down too and then walks over to the window.

"Yeah, the weather can't be beaten. It's like a vacation, sunny every day. The only time we had some rain, and it was chilly, was in January and February. But it seems the sun comes out at least once a day."

He turns to face me. "Would it be alright if I stayed with you for a while?" A smirk appears at my surprised expression.

"Uh... sure. I still have classes until the first week in May." I shrug.

"I know. Your mom told me you won't be back for Samantha and Nico's wedding." He sits cradling his coffee in his palms.

"Yeah, I have finals. You talked to my mom?"

"It was her idea for me to come here." He scrubs a hand down the front of his face, his expression pained. "I didn't mean t…"

"So now my mother's making you run after me? How embarrassing! What did she say to you?" I get up, almost causing the chair to tip over. "NO, wait. You know what? Just go home, Marco." I go into my bedroom and lock the door.

Forty-Two

VINCENT

I'VE ALWAYS HATED the smells of antiseptic in hospitals. I think my son must be used to it because he spends half his life here. Daniel is in the hospital room with Gino, Marcella, and Vanessa. He looks so young to have his position in his scrubs with his surgeon cap on. He sees me and waves me inside.

"Gino, how are you feeling today?"

"Can't wait to get out of this hell hole." He straightens up in bed. Marcella fixes his blankets. Vanessa is sitting on a chair with a book but paying more attention to Daniel than the pages. I smile to myself, knowing full well the impact my sons have on the poor defenseless women of the world. Daniel could do worse. Vanessa is gorgeous, just like her mother. They could be mistaken for sisters. Daniel is partial to blonds.

"Settle in, for now, Mr. Fiori. We have many tests to do before surgery." Daniel adjusts his stethoscope on his neck.

"How many times do I have to tell you? Call me Gino." He waves his hand in the air.

Daniel grins. "Sorry, Gino. I'll check back with you later on rounds. Does anyone need anything?"

"No, thank you." They all answer in unison.

"Great. Dad, can I speak to you for a second?" Daniel gestures with his head for me to follow him out. We go into the hall, and I close the door behind me.

"I'm taking a dinner break in twenty minutes. Meet me downstairs and join me?"

"Sure, son. I need to talk anyway."

When I return to the room, Vanessa is in the bathroom for a minute and then says goodbye and leaves. Marcella, Gino, and I have small talk until it's time for me to meet Daniel. Over the years since Tony and Marco have been such close friends, we've been in touch. Not social friends but amicable for the sake of the boys. I wanted to visit in honor of Marco so that his dad sees me as an ally. A Fiori is someone you always want on your good side.

In the lobby, the elevator doors open to a cozy scene. Vanessa's hand is on Daniel's arm as they both laugh at something. I slip out into the adjacent hallway so as not to interrupt. As soon as Vanessa presses the elevator button to return upstairs, I go to seek out my son. He interprets my smile and heads my inquiries off at the pass.

"Yes, Van is beautiful. But too innocent for my taste. I was just being nice."

Daniel and I decide to go to Tufano for dinner. It's fast and delicious. We sit across from each other, sipping our water until the waitress brings the wine.

"Dominic tells me you've gotten entangled into some sticky shit." He takes a sip of his wine.

"You could say that, son. Don Fiori is calling in a favor for saving the company from a takeover. It's important to try and keep Gino alive at all costs."

"That's the problem. Gino's brain tumor is virtually inoperable. I'm biding time by taking tests and getting his blood pressure just right. But it's a crapshoot." He finishes that sentence with a shrug.

"I cannot divulge the reason, but Don Fiori refuses to have Marco be next in line. He wants me to accept the position." I squeeze my glass tighter and take a healthy sip.

"Seriously? How do you feel about that?" Daniel's face drops.

"Like a tsunami just came in and washed away my whole world as I know it. If only Gino was well and could live a long life. Vanessa could bear a child to be the next boss."

Daniel scrubs both hands over his face, inhaling and exhaling forcefully. "I wouldn't count on Gino between me and you, dad. I'm sorry." Then he shakes his head.

I swallow. "What's the percentage, son?"

"If I can get Dr. Centoni to consult or even assist on the surgery, we have a fifty-fifty chance. If he can't adjust his schedule… not good."

"So, you wait until his schedule opens?"

"I'll ask if they want to do that. But the longer we wait, the larger the tumor gets." He exhales strongly through his teeth. "Centoni seems to think we can wait." He shrugs with his hands.

"Then wait. Any way you can up Gino's percentage, take it." The aroma of the Veal Vesuvio wafts under my nose when the waiter delivers our meals.

Forty-Three

MARCO

Fuck! I knew as soon as I said it was her mom's idea, she would take it the wrong way. I guess I really haven't given her reason to believe I have the kind of real feelings I've gathered over the past few months. Not only do I want to protect and care for her like my own family. But I'm also in love with her. There's always been a magnetic field drawing me in.

To my surprise, the door to her bedroom opens. I turn from staring out the window, and she walks up to me. Her big soulful eyes search mine.

"That was immature of me to run away. Here I'm always trying to dismiss our age difference, and then I go and do childish things. I'm sorry."

"Please don't apologize. If anyone should, it's me. For not being honest with you about what's going on in my head all this time. That's what your mom suggested I come to reveal to you, and as usual, she's right." I cup her shoulders with my hands and look straight into her eyes. "The most important is that I'm in love with you. I've always been. Not as a brother protecting you or a friend, as in my girl. The one that's on my mind when I awaken in the morning. Before I go to sleep at night. You're the first one I want to call when I have news, the one I picture myself sharing all the things I've worked so hard for in my life."

Tears are about to break free from her bottom lashes. And her hands have found their way to rest on my waist. She hooks her fingers into my belt and pulls my body into hers. My forehead touches hers, the warmth of her breath tickling my skin. It's been too long since I've inhaled her intoxicating scent of lavender and jasmine. I don't think my willpower can withstand this torture any longer. All I want is to be inside of her. Making love to every inch of her curvy body and her soft skin against my lips is my nirvana.

"For now, that's everything and all I need to know." She crashes her lips against mine, so ready to give me it all. *Can I? In good conscience, take it?* My hands run up and down her spine, causing her head to fall back. The soft expanse of her slender neck beckons to me for attention. A quivering breath escapes her mouth. I reach down to grasp the back of her legs, lifting and spreading them around my waist. Her feet and wrists lock behind me for the trip into her bedroom. My tee, along with the sundress she's wearing, ride up. It leaves only her panties between my stomach and her heat. Our lips connect the whole time.

Mimi sits up and removes her dress over her head when I place her onto the bed. Her eyes are dark with lust and crazed with a need that I can't deny. I reach back and remove my tee over my head. Then unbuckle, unzip, and let my jeans fall to the floor. My underwear follows, and her eyes go straight for my center, she reaches out to stroke me, and it's incredible. But I stay on the course and put her needs before my own. My lips sear a path down her stomach as my fingers hook her panties and remove them. Mimi's taught stomach clenches with every lick and kiss. I suck on two middle fingers and dip them inside of her divine wetness. Her hips rock against my ministrations, and she gasps, letting go for the first time. I use my mouth and tongue to bring her to climax two additional times. She's languid. Pliable in my arms as I kiss her neck from behind. She rolls over within my grasp, palming my face.

"I'm in love with you too. I want you to make love to me, to be my first, my last, and always. I'm ready now, and you sure can't hide that you are too. So, show me, teach me, make love to me." She kisses me, her hands stroking and rubbing.

"We can't because I don't have a condom."

She pushes me over onto my back and straddles my waist. Her breasts are lovely at my eye level. The sensation of the warmth and wetness of her core against my skin makes me like a steel rod.

"I'm on the pill for my periods, and you know I'm a virgin. I assume you're safe? Yes?"

"I've never had sex without a condom, so I'm safe. But…"

"Don't start overthinking this! You said when I know I'm in love is when I should do it. Well. I know." She bends over, her breasts rubbing my chest, and kisses me. "You told me you're in love with me. Show me. Make love to me, Marco."

I wrap my arms around her and flip us over, balancing on top along her body. She's so beautiful looking up at me. Starting slowly, I nibble at her breasts and neck moving downward. She's already making little mewling sounds and arching her back when I check her lubrication. There's no doubt the three previous orgasms have prepared her as much as we can.

Forty-Four

MIMI

AS HE DRANK in my desire, I gripped his shoulders, digging my nails into his skin. The man is a sex god with knowing how to use his mouth. Three times I screamed as an intense euphoria reverberated throughout my body. Now, all I can think of is having him inside of me. After convincing him it's the right time, we are at the door of the airplane thirty thousand feet in the air and ready to jump. I actually convinced him to jump without a parachute.

"It will burn a little the first time, little one. But I'll go slow. After that, it's gonna feel so good." He kisses me softly.

"If it feels half as good as before, it will be amazing." I smile as I feel his hardness against my opening. "Kiss me more." I spread my legs as wide as I can to accept him inside of me. He inches in slowly, asking if I'm okay in between kisses. *It burns a little.* I think to myself. *Let's just rip the band-aid off.* Then I grab his ass and push him into me, stretching me open he pauses, allowing me to adjust to his size, and then starts to move.

"Ahh!"

"Fuck! Meems, you're in a hurry. It feels incredible. Are you okay?"

My nails sink into his butt until a warmth spreads through me, and the friction makes it even more glorious. My hips lift in unison with his as we move together, our bodies in sync. I can feel his love for me in the tenderness of his touch, his reverence in the way he looks at me, and his devotion in the words spoken to me. Ever since the day I walked into the mansion, I felt our new connection. My thighs tense, and his legs stiffen as his movements become more frenzied. So deep he delves that an explosion happens within my core making my muscles squeeze him to his own climax. The view of his chiseled jawline and neck muscles flexed in euphoria makes my own orgasm even better. *So hot. Can't wait to see that again.*

We fall asleep in each other's arms, and I wake up at midnight. Marco is missing from my bed, but the glorious aroma of his famous grilled cheese sandwiches fills the condo. He used to make them for me after school when my mom worked late at the office with my dad. The secret is to use lots of real butter on the bread and two slices of cheese. I throw on his tee and follow my nose into the kitchen.

"That smells heavenly. I'm starving." I close my eyes, sniffing the pan.

"Me too. They're almost done. Chips on the side?" He holds up the bag.

"Did you need to ask?" I giggle.

I sit on the sofa, tuck my feet under me with a blanket across my lap. Marco hands me my plate and sits next to me. Having worked up a serious appetite, he finishes first.

"We still need to talk about some stuff." He wipes his mouth and hands with his napkin and sits facing me. "You obviously know about my sister, and I want to talk about it with you."

I nod. "I'm so sorry for blurting out.."

"No. That's not what I want to talk about. You were upset, and it was natural to say stuff you don't mean. Don't give that another thought." He takes my hand in his. "It's important to me to tell you my feelings about what happened to my sister. While you've been gone, I've seen a therapist and gone through all the steps. She says it helps to talk about it with the people you love."

All I can think about is that Julia probably wasn't really Marco's sister after hearing what Don Fiori told my dad. But I love Marco. There's nothing else I can do right now but be supportive. It's too dangerous to reveal the truth.

"I'm here to listen to whatever you need to talk about. I always will be."

He snuggles me into his arms, and I spread the blanket over both of us. "Julia was only an infant, just able to crawl all over the place. We told the nanny that she was fast and to never take her eyes off of her." He clears his throat. "I was finished for the day at school, and it was a rule that I go straight home afterward. That day some of the guys were fooling around down by the creek on our walk home. I hung around with them and lost track of time. When one guy said the time, I ran the rest of the way home and entered through the back gate. The dog was barking like crazy. What I saw will be burned into my brain for the rest of my life." He wipes his face with his palms. "Her little body was at the bottom of the pool. At first, I thought, I got this. Tony and I always dove for coins at the deep end." He shakes his head. "It happened so fast. I dropped my backpack and dove in, swimming with all I had to get to her. My fingers grabbed onto the collar of her onesie. I got to the surface with her in my arms. As soon as I laid her on the ground, I screamed her name. The nanny heard me and called the ambulance. I was almost eight years old and didn't know CPR. But I did know that if I came straight home from school that day, she might have been alive today."

I turn in his arms to face him. "Marco, you can't beat yourself up about that. There's no way to know. And the past can never be changed. We have to accept our fate and move on."

He takes my face in his hands. "That's what I've finally accepted in therapy. You've known all along just what I needed to do, Meems. You're as inciteful as your mother, and it makes me love you even more if that's even possible."

"I'm not sure that's what a girl wants to hear from her guy as a compliment... but I guess I'll take it for now." I chuckle and rub my lips against his.

"Mama D has helped me with so many weird things that have happened since you've left. It's nice to have someone to listen, and even if she has no advice, I've vented my thoughts."

"What else is going on? I lay my head back on his shoulder.

"I went to visit gram with Clyde." He twirls my hair around his fingers.

"I miss Clyde."

We both chuckle. "Me too. I'm sure he's happy as a clam with your mom and dad."

"Oh no, he'll really be spoiled when you get him back."

"So, gram said something more strange than usual this time."

"What?"

He stops twirling, and there's a pause. "She accused my dad of killing my mom."

I sit up, my mouth opens wide, eyebrows toward the ceiling. "Aa... nd what did you think of that accusation?"

"She always tells me stories about when my mom and dad were young. If I had to piece them together, it would lead me to believe that my mom loved two guys and ended up picking my dad. Which in Nana's opinion was the wrong one." He shrugs.

"My parents were told that it was an accidental overdose. I assume your mom was on meds to help her through the trauma of Julia's death?" I grab his hand.

"Yeah, that's what I'd prefer to think." He shakes his head. "My dad brought up suicide once, though."

"The cops would have known. Right?" My head tilts.

"They would say what my grandfather told them to say. We'll probably never know."

"Your grandfather has that much power, huh? My dad eluded to that when he told me about the extortion."

"I never really brought it up to you or your family because it's not something I'm proud of. I was happy with running my own business and not being included in the council activities."

"I'm sorry, babe. I wish you had more answers." I kiss him on the cheek, chin, and forehead. He cradles me back in his arms under the blanket. His scent of sandalwood and seawater relaxes me.

We end up falling asleep on the sofa, and I miss my alarm. Since my first class is over by when we wake, playing hooky it is.

Forty-Five

MARCO

In Sedona the next day, the sun is a fireball in a cloudless sky. While driving in, I couldn't help but feel like we were on another planet. The red rock buttes, all around us, are mesmerizing. We cram in as much as we can. The hike in Red Rock State Park takes up most of the morning. Then we shop in uptown Sedona and stop for lunch with incredible mountain views while we eat. There're all kinds of stores with precious stones, trinkets, and souvenirs. Afterward, we rent mountain bikes to see Oak Creek Canyon. Mimi complains of saddle sores. *I'll take care of that later.*

In the car on the drive back to the condo, Mimi is napping at my side. Her long lashes lie upon her rosy sun-kissed cheeks. She has her hair twisted up in one of those concoctions she perches on top of her head, and there's a hint of a smile on her bowed sweet lips. All I can think about is getting her back to the condo and ravishing her. You would think that I'd be tired after all the activities and driving we did today, but I'm invigorated instead.

Mimi's awake by the time we pull into the parking lot. She claims she can't wait to go to the bathroom, jumps out of the car, and runs up the stairs. As I get our backpacks and water bottles out of the car, I notice a gardenia bush blooming next to her parking place. Not being able to resist, I pick a couple to bring inside. They smell amazing. I put all the stuff down in the kitchen. When I enter the bedroom, the sight before me is captivating. Mimi's hair is fanned out above her on the pale pink comforter. Her legs are spread, knees bent, and her fingers dipped between them. I lick my lips as she distributes her wetness to her nub and moans.

"Holy shit, Meems! Are you trying to give me a heart attack?"

"I was hoping I would affect you in a little lower region." She bites her bottom lip.

"I brought you something." I hide the flowers behind my back and walk over to the bed.

"What is it?" Her voice is breathy. One in each hand, I seductively trace her nipples with the petals of the gardenia. "That smells heavenly."

I reach back and grab my tee over my head. Then whip off my pants and boxers. My eyes follow her fingers, swirling faster, skin flushing with need. I'm as hard as fucking steel. One of her feet hook around my knee and pull me out of my stupor. After a deep inhale, I grab her ankles, pulling her to the edge of the bed. Then I skim my hands up her calves and the backs of her thighs to my final destination, two handfuls of this ass. She moans when I squeeze, opening her up totally to my gaze and my mouth. Almost immediately, she climaxes long and hard. I lean over and penetrate slowly, kissing her to keep her mind occupied in case there's still any pain. Low sounds of pleasure come from the back of her throat, indicating that's not the case. For her to want me bare sinking into her wet heat makes our union all the more special. It's a first for me too.

"Fuck, the way you feel is mind-blowing." All the emotions of finally being with her this way hits me at once. Her sighs and moans of satisfaction, the strokes, and loving caresses, and the warm tight connection joining us as one. This is my world. Amelia is my world.

After two blissful weeks in Arizona, while Mimi finishes up with school were sitting on the balcony dialing Daniel for an update on my father.

"Hey Buddy, how's he doing today?" I pull Meems onto my lap.

"Still no change in his test results. He's no closer to getting surgery than the day you left. I'm switching up some of his meds, and we'll see how that fares in two days. It's kinda like walking a tight rope keeping him stable enough for surgery without danger of a stroke."

"How's he holding up mentally?"

"His wife and Vanessa are keeping him occupied. But being in the hospital this long is daunting. You should call him again."

"I will as soon as I hang up with you."

"When are you coming home? We missed you both at Samantha and Nico's wedding."

"So, you and your brothers are not gonna have me whacked for having your sister as my girlfriend when I get back?" Mimi rolls her eyes.

"Fuck no. Listen, bro, mom told all of us at Sunday dinner together."

I clear my throat. "Mama D was dying to tell everyone. I couldn't stop her if I tried. I wanted to talk to your dad myself, but she said it wasn't necessary."

"We all cracked up cause' we knew, for years, you two would someday get together. There's nobody better to take good care of our sister." I kiss her on the forehead.

"That's right!" Mimi shouts into the phone. "We'll be back for Sunday dinner next week."

"Great, I'll make sure to be there. Marco, I'll text you about the blood results."

"Thanks, bro. See you soon." I hang up the phone and hug my girl. Then we call my father's room.

Forty-Six

AMELIA

IT'S good to be back home, except I'm alone in my bed. The humidity in Illinois takes getting used to after months in Arizona. I've felt a little dizzy at times and nauseous. The morning outside looks bright and inviting. But I'm not feeling myself. All I can do is push forward and hope I acclimate soon.

Marco and I have been working nonstop on a new project together. There's a great opportunity that fell into our lap the week we got back to chi town. A condo in Marco's building came up in foreclosure. The owner approached him with a bargain-basement low price, so they didn't lose it all. He took it as is. Since then, renovations have consumed us for five weeks since we came back. Marco fits in visits with his dad. Gino survived the brain surgery and now convalesces at home. My brother Daniel is a hero. Being one of the two surgeons to remove Gino's tumor, the accolades belong to him.

The phone blows up on my nightstand next to me. It's Alex. When I sit up too fast, I get dizzy.

"Hello, stranger."

"Tony just happened to mention you're home from school. How's it goin'?"

The photographs Alex took of me made him some money at the

gallery. But he's using all his time now at the company creating new gaming software. Tony told me I found him a genius in disguise.

"Yeah, been back about five weeks. Working on a new project."

"How about getting a coffee with me one day soon and catch up. I wanna show you the results of the gallery show." It sounds like he's sucking on his signature cigarette.

"Okay, maybe one day next week?" I run my finger over the spine of my latest read next to me on the bed.

"How's Friday after work?"

"Maybe. I'll text you for sure tomorrow."

"Great. See ya."

My mom calls me downstairs as soon as I hang up. She's at the kitchen table with a tablet and pen writing furiously.

"What's up, ma?" I peer over her shoulder.

"I'm making a guest list for a surprise fiftieth birthday party for your father. Will you help with the arrangements?" She looks back at me and smiles.

"Sure, that sounds fun. When is it?" I grab the chair across from her.

"The week before his actual birthday, so he won't even remember it's here." She chuckles. "I'm going to need you and your brothers to greet everyone and make sure the caterers have all the food ready here. Then you'll need to call us in Lake Geneva two hours before the party starts with some reason why we need to come home. Any ideas?"

"How about someone broke in? Or I'm sick? Or... um..." I look up at the ceiling.

"I don't want him scared and driving like a maniac, so can we come up with a clever reason that's not an emergency, but we're needed at home?"

"I know! How about the hot water heater broke and waters all over the place?" I shrug.

"No, I'd be able to handle that for your parents, and your dad knows it." Marco walks in from the hallway by the garage with Clyde in his arms. I jump up and put my arms around his neck, with Clyde licking my chin between us.

"How do you know what we're talking about, Mr.?

"Mama D and I were trying to come up with ideas the other day for the same thing. I came up with a great one this morning." His eyes sparkle with mischief.

"What is it, Marco!" Mom sits up, eyes wide.

"I'll ask for his blessing before you leave to ask Mimi to marry me. Then, we'll fake our impromptu engagement party, so you guys will have to come home." He shrugs.

"Perfect! Mom says. She jumps up and hugs him.

I look up into Marco's face with a smirk. "Wow, don't hold back as to what's been on your mind, sir. A fake engagement?" I turn and sit back in the chair, one leg tucked underneath me. "Does that mean I get a fake ring?" I giggle.

"There's no need for a ring because, by the time your dad sees you, we'll already have yelled surprise." He smiles big like he's got it all figured out.

"Oh, good planning." I stick out my bottom lip dramatically. Marco laughs. He hands Clyde to me and opens the frig, takes out the mayo and lunchmeat. I get up, switching Clyde into my left hand, and give him the bread with my right.

"Now that our plan is made, will you both help me with invitations?" Mom takes a bag out from under the table and pulls out a stack of invites.

"Why don't you use evites?" Marco asks.

I roll my eyes. "Are you kidding? Their generation only does it this way. Hurry up and eat so you can help stuff the envelopes."

"Yes, boss." He kisses me on the head. My mom grins from ear to ear. "This is a pretty large list with all the employees from Dragon included."

"It's a milestone birthday for daddy, and I wanted to include all his friends from work. If you include one, you must include them all. It's only proper. I stipulated 'no gifts' on the invitation purposely. The celebration is just to acknowledge and appreciate another year for your father."

Forty-Seven

MARCO

THE RING IS STUNNING when I pick it up at the jeweler. It's slightly over two carats in a brilliant cut on a simple diamond-studded band. Mimi's hands are so petite like the rest of her the ring will look just perfect. No one knows that the fake engagement is going to actually be real. God knows no man wants to go through this stress twice on purpose. My nerves are shot. Vince and Mama D are leaving for Lake Geneva this afternoon, and my next step is to ask for their blessing. I made sure to send Mimi on an errand for the job so just her parents would be at home. Mama D cured my anxiety before I left for Arizona about my relationship with Amelia. But marriage might be a different thing altogether. She's gonna flip when I show her the ring.

Vincent looks more rested than the last time I saw him. He and Mama D are getting stuff ready for the trip to Lake Geneva for the weekend. She winks at me as I enter the kitchen.

"Hey, you two, can I have a word with both of you? Come sit on the sofa with me for a minute." They both follow my lead, and we all sit with me in the middle. It's so much better that way, so I don't have to face anyone directly.

"Everything alright, son?" Vincent asks.

"All good. I just want to take this opportunity to tell you both how much I love this family."

"We love you t…"

"I know, I know." I put a hand on each of their knees. "Please let me just tell you what I need to first, and then you can answer after. Okay?" They both nod, grinning.

I explode a breath through my lips and continue. "So, I love this family, but also I'm *in* love with Amelia. I would like your blessing to make her my wife and spend the rest of my life making her happy."

Vincent gets up, and Lucia looks at me with tears in her eyes. She can feel that it's real because she knows me so well. Mama D never misses a thing. She can sense how nervous I am and knows if it was fake, that wouldn't be the case.

"We love you, son. Of course, you have our blessing." He holds out his hand, and I stand to shake it when he pulls me into a hug. Mama D gets in on the hug, and we all laugh.

"You wanna see the ring?" I pull it out of my pocket and open the velvet box.

"Oh, Marco! It's lovely! I'm so excited. When will you ask her?"

"She'll love it, son." Vincent takes the box from Lucia.

"No plans yet. Be ready for a screaming phone call at any time."

This is like the best of both worlds for me. It's like asking Mimi's parents for their blessing and telling my parents the news in one fell sweep. I know I'll have to call my father and Marcella, but it can wait until after I ask Mimi. We'll call together.

After they leave, I'm still kinda revved up, so I grab a beer from the frig and wait for Meems to get home. I can't sit still long enough to watch television, so I pace. The ring just might burn a hole in my pocket. I might have to ask her tonight.

The door to the garage opens, and there she is, jeans painted on that petite frame. I stand up, arms out to make her run to me. No words, she kicks off her heels and runs. One bare foot on my bent knee, a jump, the other wrapped around my waist, and finally, her ankles and wrists locked behind me. Climbs me just like a tree, my little nymph.

"Hey." She smirks, and I can tell the smoldering thoughts running through her mind.

"Hey, little one. How bout' a kiss?" I pucker at her.

"How bout' you walk us on up to my bedroom, and we have many kisses?" She winks.

"How do you know we're alone?" I can't help but smile.

"I already talked to my mother, they are halfway to the lake house."

I walk toward the stairs. "Clever little nymph, aren't you?" She throws her head back, laughing.

"Yes, I am."

She fiddles with the buttons on my shirt with one hand and holds on with the other. Her breath on my neck and fingers on my pecks barely leave me the strength to get us to the second level. Once in her room, I kick the door closed and drop her on the bed. She unzips her jeans, and I peel them off along with her panties. She makes quick work of her tank and bra. She is more beautiful than any woman I've ever laid eyes on. Her skin is flawless and tan, her breasts full and round with garnet nipples just waiting for my attention. When my jeans hit the floor, her eyes focus on my arousal, and that sexy tongue swipes her bottom lip. She gives me the come-hither index finger, and I'm done for.

Forty-Eight

MIMI

MARCO STANDS next to the bed, naked, for a few seconds to admire me. I relish the feeling of his eyes on me, filled with lust and devotion. That look on his face sends my heartbeat into revelry like the morning trumpet to wake the troops. It's familiar in its veiled haze. I've seen it many times between my parents or Sam and Nico. Pure unconditional love. The kind of love that lasts forever, and all I want to do is bask in it.

But I can't wait another second. When I signal to get over here, it breaks Marco's trance, and he kneels over me. He slowly lathes his lips and tongue around my nipples, tugging on the invisible connection between breast and core. My womb clenches and my back arches up toward him. His hands drift up and down my body, tickling my senses and driving me wild. Until finally, his fingers slither inside right where I long them to be. He's stretching them, forcing my composure to crack, giving way to the hunger. My body tightens, and our movements quicken under his erotic direction until I convulse on the covers.

"You're so ready for me, Meems.

"Now, please… I need you." I scream as he positions himself.

My toes curl as I give myself over to ecstasy. There's nothing sexier than the sight above me, and I struggle to keep my eyes open to witness the beauty. The muscles in his neck are corded and strained, leading up to his strong chiseled jaw and sexy lips. As the sweat gathers on his forehead, his eyes are lost in a fiery haze. The sounds that come out of his mouth with each thrust are deep and raw. The bed slams back against the wall, the sheets are crumpled in my fists. We both climax as my muscles tighten, pulling him over the edge right with me.

He plops on his side next to me, and his arms pull me closer. My head is under his chin as he lazily runs an index finger up and down my spine. His voice is a whisper right above my ear.

"Since the first time I laid eyes on you, the sun shone again in my life. When your mom made me wash my hands and then put you into my arms, it was like your soul spoke to mine. You were so small, maybe six or seven pounds, but your eyes held me captive. I could look at you all day…especially after you grabbed my finger in your little fist. You held on for dear life." I turn in his arms and wipe the tears from my cheeks at his heartfelt words. He reaches for something on the floor in front of my nightstand. "That's what I want to do now. I wanna hold on to *you* for dear life. I want to grab onto this finger and claim it as mine." He takes my left ring finger and places a gorgeous diamond engagement ring on it. "Will you be my wife, little one?"

I pop up to the sitting position staring at the ring. "Marco, is this real or to pull off my father's surprise party?"

"It's as real as the ring on your finger and the love in my heart."

"OH, my gosh!" I jump on him, kissing his whole face, smashing my lips against his as hard as I can.

"Hmm… mmm…is...that…mmm…a yes?" Marco's eyes search mine, our lips still stuck together.

"YES! Yes, I will be your wife, and you will be my husband. Yes!"

After another toe-curling session of lovemaking, we lay there more in love than ever. Minutes and heartbeats fly silently by for a time in each other's arms. Then Marco's head pops up, and I look up at him.

"I left out the most important thing! I love you, little one."

"I love you too." I reach up and kiss him. "You thought I was a pretty cute baby, huh?

He chuckles and pinches my butt cheek. "I still think your pretty cute."

Forty-Nine

VINCENT

WE DON'T ARRIVE at the summer home in Lake Geneva, Wisconsin, until four-thirty. I'm starving because we decided to wait and just have an early dinner here. Lucia gets busy in the kitchen making some pork chops, and I put away the stuff we brought up from home. After we eat, the evening is tranquil. We sit on the back porch overlooking the water with our limoncello.

"Aren't you excited to be planning a wedding soon?"

"I can't believe our wish finally came true. The whole family knew they have always been meant for each other except the two of them." Lucia sips her drink.

We've indeed seen it many times over the years. Marco and Amelia with their heads together whispering. Always offering to help each other with chores. Sticking up for each other when the other boys would pick on one of them. My phone vibrates on the table between the two lounge chairs. The kids always call my phone first because Lucia never charges hers. I press the green button to accept a video call. We both can see and hear Amelia; Marco is behind her.

"Hey, sweetie, what's up?"

"Hiiii, guess what! Marco asked me to marry him." She holds up her hand and shows us the ring on her finger. Then she jumps up and down with excitement.

"Congratulations, you two! We're so happy for both of you."

"You guys have to come home tomorrow. We invited everyone for an engagement celebration. Mom, you don't have to do a thing. I ordered caterers, and Tony will bartend."

"Oh, honey, that's great because it would be difficult to get home in time for me to cook. What time is everyone coming?"

"We said seven." She claps her hands.

"We will be there in time. We're so happy for you both. We love you." Lucia wipes a tear from her cheek.

"Did you two call Anthony and Liz? Dominic and Daniel? Gino and Marcella?" I ask, cradling my wife in my arms in front of me so they can see us both.

"We're about to do that now. So, we'll see you tomorrow. Love you both too." Our daughter is beaming when she blows us kisses to say goodbye.

We settle into the same lounge chair after the phone call. My wife in my arms looking at the stars is where I always feel happiest.

Our house is buzzing with guests when I walk in with my wife the next day. Everyone yells surprise for my fiftieth birthday milestone. I'm shocked and honored that the party was planned for me, but I am proud to share the celebration with my daughter and Marco. The whole family is here with friends and even work associates.

Don Fiori is the only guest who doesn't greet me at the door. I am summoned into my own home office, where he sits in the wing-back chair next to my bar cart. There are two glasses of anisette on the table between the chairs when I sit opposite him. He picks his up and toasts.

"Salute Vincenzo on your birthday and to our ongoing arrangement. I wish us all luck together in the future."

We both drink our shots, and he gestures for me to fill the glasses again. "Salute to your daughter Amelia and my grandson Marco on their engagement."

"Thank you, Don Fiori."

"It's too bad my whore of a daughter-in-law made a fatal mistake. When your daughter has a child, we would have had a blood heir between our families. If only Marco was Gino's biological son. We…"

His phone rings interrupting his sentence.

I just nod, finding myself speechless at his words. Since I've taken the oath of silence, I promised to guard any information regarding the Fiori family with my life.

Little did we know, this night would change the dynamic of our Dragonetti family forever. It is disappointing for me because it turns out to be day *one* of the reluctant repayment of my debt to Don Fiori.

Fifty

MARCO

THE HOUSE IS full of laughter, music, and good food. I can't remember the last time I was this happy. My girl is in my arms as we sway together to Sinatra Vincent's favorite for dinner party music. His other tastes are the opposite end of the music spectrum, like AC/DC. He's always been a cool guy and has treated me like a son, Amelia, and I will never have in-law problems. My dad is never around, and Marcella is too young to play the nasty mother-in-law. *I wonder why they haven't arrived yet.*

"Hey, sweetie, how come your dad isn't here yet?" Mimi asks, reading my mind.

"I don't know. I wonder if he wasn't feeling well. Gino's been fine the last few weeks, so he was anxious to come tonight. Maybe I'll text them."

The text goes unanswered.

A few minutes later, Sam, one of my grandfather's bodyguards, comes out on the terrace to call us into Vince's office. My grandfather is sitting in one of the wingback chairs with his head in his hands. I've never seen this man like this. But as soon as he realizes we've entered, he resumes his usual intimidating demeanor. The infamous Don Fiori straightens his spine and raises his chin. He looks much older than the last time I saw him. I can't remember how long it's been.

"Marco, please sit," He summons me.

Amelia lets go of my hand and steps over to where her father is near the window. He pulls out his desk chair for her to sit, and with his hands lovingly on her shoulders, he stands behind her.

"There has been an accident. Your father and Marcella were fatally injured, and the perpetrator fled the scene." My daunting grandfather discloses the information as if he's a news reporter.

I stand up, arms outstretched. Questions fly out of my mouth in rapid succession.

"What are you saying? Are you sure they're dead? Shouldn't we go to the hospital? Where's Vanessa?"

"Sit!" I do as he says. "Vanessa is at school; she is being brought here as we speak." He rubs his hand over his mouth and chin. "I'm certain that they are dead. I've sent my men there to represent us. We cannot go to the hospital. I have reason to believe this is a power struggle to take over our family's position. With your father gone, I am the only Fiori left on the council. As head of the organization, I have deemed that you will not take my place as boss. The capos see that as a weakness within our family and a reason to try and mutiny now."

"Have you put all of us in danger here?" I gesture to Mimi and Vince.

"It has always been my intention to keep you out of the business. Safe from all the violence and greed, but I'm sorry to say that I might have failed. There's protection ordered for all of you. Especially since your father had his brain tumor, I have named Vincenzo will be boss when I'm gone. Gino would have been my successor but now."

His voice trails off. My head spins. I squeeze my eyes shut for one second, trying desperately to make sense of things. Why my father would live through a brain tumor, life-threatening surgery, and all his rehabilitation just to die this way so soon. My dad is dead. Even though we were never close, I feel empty inside. Both my parents and Julia are gone. This leaves me with only my grandfather and Vanessa in my immediate family. Amelia's soft touch on my arm reminds me that I'm never alone. I have my family here. Blood is fine, but it's not necessary for the bond of family.

Fifty-One

AMELIA

Rain, storms, and more rain. The streets are flooded throughout Illinois to the point where you can use a boat. Pictures on the news of Elmhurst, where my cousins live, have what looks like rapids going down the main street. The famous hot dog place my dad loves is underwater again too.

The last few days have been grueling. The crowded funeral for Marco's father and Marcella took a lot of energy to get through. Cars lined up in procession from the funeral home to the cemetery for miles. After the luncheon, I went back to my house, and Marco took Vanessa home with him. She decided to take him up on his offer to live with him until she gets on her feet.

I find my dad in his office and curl up in one of his chairs beside his desk.

"Isn't it creepy that the people responsible for their deaths might have been in attendance?" I put my hair up in a ponytail to get more comfortable.

"Everyone must pay their respects, or they look guilty. All the families were represented by the capos except Ricci's. Pietro Ricci, the retired capo of their family, came instead of Alberto Ricci, his son. It was made known that Alberto is in Italy for a personal matter." My dad leans back in his chair, giving me his full attention.

"So, do you think Alberto had anything to do with the murders?"

Dad scratches his head and grimaces. "I don't like to speculate. Don Fiori once told me that he and Don Pietro went to school together and were childhood friends. Maybe that's why it was acceptable for the old man to come instead of the capo. Who knows?" He shrugs.

"How do you feel now that you are next in line instead of third?" I pick up the paperweight and turn it over in my hand.

"It's daunting, to say the least. I have no choice. Like I was telling your mother, you can't say no to Don Fiori. I keep thinking I'm somehow gonna find a way out of it before I have to step up." He wipes his hands down his face.

"Do you blame Marco, daddy?"

"Never, sweetie, I did this myself by asking the Don for help with the extortionists. Some days I think it might have been safer to pay them." He chuckles, shaking his head slowly.

"Yeah, maybe." I get up from the chair and bend to hug my dad. "I'm going over by Marco to try and make Vanessa feel better and hang out."

"Okay, sweetie. Be careful take Sam with you."

"I will. bye, daddy." I kiss his cheek.

It's weird somebody driving me everywhere I go now. Having a bodyguard is something I'd never believed possible for someone like me. Sam is nice. He's a little older than Marco but not as old as my dad. He's usually my dad's guy unless he's at home. Then Sam's with me. Or mom. On other days, I've had Keith, who seems like an ad for Ritalin, but who am I to judge.

When I get to Marco's, Sam hangs with his guy Shaun in the hallway. I step inside to the aroma of pizza.

"Something smells yummy!" Marco holds out his arms, and I jump into them. He kisses me like I'm the last of his favorite cookies on the platter.

"I can't wait to find someone who will love me like that." Vanessa is leaning against the doorframe to the guest room. Her smile is wide.

I giggle, and Marco lets me down. "You will, someday, sweetie."

"How did you know that it's the real thing? What's so different from the other people you've dated?" She walks into the kitchen, her head tilted.

Marco stands by the island and opens the pizza box. He hands us all paper plates. "You just know by the way you feel when that person is around compared to when they're not." He sits and takes a bite of pizza, so I elaborate.

"Your person is the one that you think about constantly. You wake up with them on your mind and go to sleep the same. They are the person who loves you unconditionally without judgment or ridicule. They are patient and protective." I smile at Marco, and his lustful expression makes me sweat.

He gets up and pulls me from my chair. While holding me at arm's length, his eyes travel my body up and down. "It's the person who makes you crazy hot just looking at them." Then he spins me in a circle.

Vanessa giggles. "You guys are so cute. When's the wedding?" She takes a big bite.

"Well, since Liz and Tony are getting married in Vegas in two weeks, we can pick a date after that. We wanted to wait until after they finally tied the knot," Marco says.

"Tony's finally back from his work travel for a while, and he now has Alex Greyson taking over some stuff to free up his time. What a great fit sending him to work with my brother. I should introduce you to him. He's your age."

"Why isn't he still in college?" Van uses her napkin to wipe the tomato sauce on her chin.

"His parents are both gone. But Tony says he's smart and talented."

We finish the pizza, and Vanessa gets a box out of her room with the poster she made for her mom and dad's funeral. She wanted to portray their lives in pictures for the people to look at during the wake. I sit down and help her carefully remove each snapshot, placing them back into her parents' box. A particular photo jumps out at me, giving me goosebumps all over my body. I don't want to be obvious, so I palm the pic and excuse myself to the bathroom for a closer look.

Marco's watching the Cubs on television, and I close the door softly not to disturb him. I bring the image up under the overhead lights for a closer look. Marco's father and mother are teenagers with another guy. They have their arms around each other, posing together with big smiles. I recognize his dad Gino, but weirdly the other guy is almost an exact clone of Marco. *The secret my dad told me about Marco's birth mother might be making me sense the resemblance? How come no one else ever noticed this? Has this picture been hidden away? Who is this man, and maybe he is Marco's biological father?*

I decide to keep the picture and show my father before returning it.

Fifty-Two

MARCO

Tony and I have been more like brothers than best friends since we were in kindergarten. I'm honored that he decided to ask me to be his best man for his wedding. It saved him from choosing between his twin brothers. The extra bonus is Amelia is Elizabeth's maid of honor. We get to walk down the aisle together before our own wedding. They opted for a small intimate ceremony with just immediate family and friends instead of the usual Dragonetti all-out bash that we'll probably have. Elizabeth wanted it simple, and according to Tony, the bride gets her day her way.

The night before the wedding, I get the guys together for a small bachelor party. We play a few practical jokes on the groom in our suite. When he takes a shower to go out on the strip, I steal all the towels from the bathroom. Needless to say, he's pissed to have to drip dry. Afterward, his brothers somehow handcuff him to a naked blow-up doll, among some other funny pranks. Tony laughs with us but vows to get every one of us back. I may regret it come to my wedding.

The next day, there's no Elvis or crazy venue. A simple little place with an altar and an aisle is perfect. The sun shines through the stained-glass windows creating a mosaic rainbow. Some religious icons fill the space with peaceful deities, and Mimi refers to the music as romantic. She looks like a beautiful angel in her light pink dress. It flows as she walks, reaching just to her sexy thighs. Her brown hair is swept up off her graceful neck, with just small pieces framing her face. That smile lights up my world as she walks toward me and takes my arm to head on up to the alter. The photographer flashes quick pics and moves on to the bride behind us. I take my place next to Tony, clapping him on the shoulder and shaking his hand. Then we watch the love of his life approach, looking happy and excited.

The reception is in an executive suite at the Bellagio with all the food and drinks you could ask for. Vince and mama D look happy and tired. By the time we all finish eating and gather at the bar, Daniel and Dominic are ready to go out on the town. If Tess bunks with her new grandparents, the bride and groom will join.

"You wanna hit the clubs with them?" Amelia sashays up to me and puts her arms around my neck.

"With you lookin' so hot and standing so close, I'm quickly changing my mind."

She playfully slaps my chest. "There's plenty of time for that later. Let's go out on the town."

I pull her into me, tight. Then I kiss her like it's the last thing I'll ever do. She still has her eyes closed when I pull back. "Did I change your mind?

"Nope. But you can try again, old man. I knew you were already too old to party." She giggles.

"You sexy little nymph, you're just trying to drive me crazy. I'll show you *too old* later."

"Yup. I'm counting on it. Let's go."

The Omnia at Ceasar's Palace is where we end up. Tony leads the way to the VIP tables, and the drinks start flowing. Daniel disappears first, catching the eye of some blond with huge tits. Dominic follows suit with another chick. The bride and groom are into each other tucked in the booth.

"Wanna dance?" Mimi grabs my lapels and pulls me on the dance floor.

"Lead the way, little one."

The music is loud, the people are sweaty, and we get bumped into repeatedly, but I can ignore all of that when my gorgeous girl sways, rubbing up against me. Her little pink dress lifts up as her hips move, and I can't wait to lick those thighs. After nonstop dancing, a sheen of moisture on her skin makes her glow under the lights. Her tongue swipes over her lips seductively. I wrap my arms around her, put my mouth by her ear so she can hear me.

"Let's go out on the patio to cool off."

She nods, and I lead the way. A cool breeze feels good on my skin as I back Mimi into a corner of the patio to kiss her.

"Ready to go back to the hotel?" I press my erection against her to show how ready I am.

"You obviously are." She giggles.

"Yup, we can order a car back and text the others. We'll see them at breakfast." I tap out the car request on the app on my phone and grab her hand to exit. In the elevator, on the way down to the lobby, Mimi sways. I put my arm around to steady her. The heels she has on are so high I don't know how women can walk in them. Don't get me wrong, I still think they're sexy as fuck.

The car is waiting out front of Ceasars, the bellhop gestures, "Mr. Fiori" and we hop in.

"I'm glad we don't have to drive. Between the champagne at the wedding and bottle service at the club, I'm pretty tipsy." Mimi puts her head on my shoulder.

"Yeah, I've had too much to drive for sure."

We relax in the back of the limo, not realizing the length of the ride is way more than back to Bellagio. The driver pulls over, stops the car, and we sit up. When I try to open the door, it won't budge.

"Hey, I can't open the…"

A disembodied voice comes over the speaker system in the car. "Open the compartment on the left side, remove the blindfolds, put them on. You are being taken to an undisclosed location. There's no reason to resist or be frightened. Do as you're told, and you will be released unharmed."

"What kind of joke is this? Did my brother Tony put you up to this?" I knock on the window separating us from the front seat.

"Do as you're told, and you will know everything soon enough." The voice gets louder.

Mimi and I look at each other and shrug. We might as well go along with the hoax. There's no way to get out of the car anyway. I just hope they don't drop us off in the middle of the desert and leave. Tony sure has arranged an act of elaborate revenge for the stupid stuff I pulled at his bachelor party.

Fifty-Three

AMELIA

"Wow, this is seriously crushing my buzz." I take the blindfolds out of the compartment and hand one to Marco. *What does my brother have up his sleeve? Whatever stupid prank this is, I hope it doesn't take long. I want my sexy time with my man.*

The material is black, so once over our eyes, we can see nothing. The car starts moving again until we hear a motorized garage door open and close above us. After the automatic locks click to the doors, on each side are men pulling us out of the seats. I don't resist because I think it's a joke.

"Where are we? Tony, is that you?" Marco?"

"Silence!" My handler braces my hands behind my back and zip ties them. This is no prank; bile starts rising in my stomach. Now I try and resist, but he's too strong for me. Marco never answered me. If he could speak, he would try to calm me.

The next thing I know, I'm put into a chair and left alone in a room. I'm shaking uncontrollably at the realization we're in some kind of danger. Who knows where my bag and phone are. Left on the seat in the limo.

The door opens with footsteps approaching me. *What are they going to do to me? Where's Marco?* "Why are you doing this? Who are you?"

"Hello, Ms. Dragonetti. Let me help you." His hands are on my hair, and I snap my head away. "No need to be afraid I want to remove the blindfold. But should you like it to remain…"

"No!"

"Then stay still, and I will remove it for you." His voice is low and raspy, with a slight accent. He enunciates his words as if English is not his only language. I try to stop shaking as he gives me back the luxury of sight. I don't want to appear weak, but I'm failing miserably.

Blink.

Blink.

Recognition.

This has to be Marco's biological father, or I'm in an alternate universe where he's a slightly older clone. It's not every day you can look into the future to see what the man you love will look like twenty years from now. Wow, I hit the gene pool jackpot to father my children. The only difference is in their eye color. *Who is this man, and does he know?*

"I apologize for the shock and awe. We needed to get you here as soon as possible. I need a snapshot." He takes my picture… with my own phone.

"Who are you? Why are you doing this?"

My questions are ignored. He puts the phone in front of my face to unlock it by facial recognition. Then types a message and pressed send.

"Who are you texting?" Where's Marco? What have you done to him? If you hurt him, you'll regret it!"

He stares down at me with a grin. If I didn't fear him, I might find myself to be attracted to this man. He still has a full thick head of hair like Marco, but a small amount of grey at the temples. Same build, same height, same facial expressions on his attractive sculpted face. His eyes are an arresting aquamarine blue, an amused sparkle in them. The only difference I can see right now.

"Sei un petardo, e una bellezza." (*You're a firecracker and a beauty.*) He steps behind me, not waiting for a reply. "All your questions will be answered in due time, Princess. You're quite safe here. I'm going to untie you now, but I need cooperation until your father gets here. Just sit and be good."

"Why are you waiting for my father? Please tell me what this is all about."

"Basta" (*Enough.*) He raises his voice, and I'm taken aback. "I'm sorry to raise my voice." He shakes his head. "It's been a difficult day, forgive me."

After he unties my hands only and leaves, an older lady brings in water and coffee with Italian cookies. I'm sure she baked them. The questions roll off my tongue. I don't think she speaks a word of English. She just shrugs and smiles, murmuring softly in Italian to calm me. It's almost as if he's treating me like a guest. Weird.

Fifty-Four

VINCENT

TESS IS EXHAUSTED when we put her to sleep in the other bedroom of our suite. I pour two glasses of champagne, and we relax for a while, enjoying the lights of the Vegas strip out our balcony. Lucia and I are in the hot tub in our suite when my phone buzzes with a message from Amelia. Only it's evident someone else has commandeered her phone.

"What is it, sweetheart? You've lost all color in your face," Lucia says.

"It's Amelia. She's been taken, and they want us to come to where she is." I grab a towel and jump out. "The message says she's safe. But it looks as if she's shaken. I can only see her face."

"What! What are we going to do?" Lucia follows.

"Let me call Don Fiori. See what he knows."

There's no getting in touch with the infamous Don, so Lucia and I get dressed. We make sure Tony and Liz are in their room in case Tess wakes up. A car is waiting when we arrive at the lobby. Not sure if this is a good idea, but my daughter is there with them, and I can't let her down. Sam, Shaun, and Keith are all in a car behind us. How they lost sight of Marco and Amelia at the club is a mystery to me. Don Fiori is still their employer, so I can't fire anyone over this. For now, I have to stay calm and hope I can talk to whoever is running this show in Vegas.

We pull up to a garage, and only our car is allowed inside. The bodyguards are of no good to us once again. The door to the limo opens, and I follow Lucia out into a parking garage. The attendant directs us without saying a word. Once the elevator doors open at the top of the building, floor-to-ceiling windows distract us with a view of the Vegas strip. We're alone until a deep voice registers from behind us. We quickly turn around.

"Welcome, Mr. and Mrs. Dragonetti."

"Where's our daughter! If you've laid one finger…"

He puts his hand up, palm facing us to shut me up as he interrupts. "I assure you, Amelia is perfectly safe and untouched. My cook is serving her coffee and cookies. She will be in shortly."

Now that I'm calmer and not seething with as much anger, I can take in who this man really is. I'll be damned if this guy isn't Marco's father and the same one in the picture Mimi found. The only sign of age is a few grey hairs. *Could that be why we're here? Because she found out his secret?*

Fifty-Five

MARCO

As soon as the doors to the car open, they separate us. Mimi is rattling off questions and then what I assume is the elevator door cuts off all sound from the garage.

"Hey, buddy, when can I take the blindfold off? Are Tony and the guys here? I can take a joke as well as the next guy, but this is making me nervous. It's kinda going above and beyond bachelor party pranks."

"Soon, just cooperate, and you'll see what this is all about."

The doors open, and the guy leads me to sit at a table. I hear a man clear his throat on the other side of the room.

"What did I tell you? He's the spitting image!" A woman says to my left.

"I believed you, Lana. What I can't fathom is how I didn't know for so long. It seems Don Fiori has been keeping this from us. All these years, my father treated the Fiori family as allies." A man answers from my right.

"Excuse me. This doesn't sound like a prank. Who are you, and what's going on here?" I rip off the blindfold. The guy I assume who brought me up from the garage puts his hands on my shoulders to keep me seated.

"I'm sorry, let me explain."

I look to my left and recognize the girl I took to lunch after the hospital. "I know you. That girl who approached me at the hospital. Lana Riley."

She waves away the man behind me and offers her hand. "Hello, again, Marco. Let me introduce you to Alberto Ricci, the man I believe to be your biological father."

I can feel my bottom lip head toward the floor. My eyebrows crush together. I turn toward the direction she gestures with her finger. *If someone orchestrated this as a prank, they did pretty well with the actors.* There's no denying the man could be my father. His features are like looking in a mirror that someone aged my reflection about twenty years. He is obviously as shocked as I am but has had more time to process this because he speaks, and I can't get one word to come out.

"It's wonderful to finally meet you. An offer to shake my hand. I don't move. You're as shocked as I am, I see."

I nod, getting up from the chair with the sudden urge to pace. My grandmother's stories are floating through my brain. *Two boys to choose between. In love with both.*

"Were you the other boy my mother dated in high school that my grandmother talks about?" I stop and stare at him, waiting for an answer.

He sits on the sofa and crosses his ankle over his knee. Lana sits on the arm next to him.

"Yes, your mother and I were in love in high school." He looks into my eyes. "You have her eyes. I was shocked and heartbroken when she, as you kids would say, ghosted me and married Gino. Whenever I called her house, her father would answer and tell me to stop calling. Her best friend would arrange meetings and phone calls for a while. But something made your mother turn against me. It was the summer after graduation, and I went away to school after that. When I returned, life resumed according to the ways of my family, and my father insisted I take my place as Capo under him. You were already born, and Mia and Gino were supposedly a happy couple. I went to live in Italy for many years, commuting back to the U.S. when needed. My father has recently taken ill, and I have moved back for him. Here we are." He puts his hands out, palms up.

"Did my father know? My grandfather?" I sit in the chair across from them.

"Marco, although this is an important subject we need to discuss. There's something else I'm dealing with right now." He leans forward and puts his elbows on his knees, clasping his hands. "I know who killed Gino and Marcella. Carmine Bonino. The Bonino's are looking to take over Don Fiori's position at the top of the five families in the council. The Don is already in hiding. It seemed important to bring you here since Gino is dead, and they still think you're his son. I have Vincent and Lucia on the way here too. Don Fiori put them in a dangerous position by naming him his successor. For the time being, they will be safe here too."

"Where's Amelia? I want to see her. Why all the blindfolds and zip ties?"

"She's with her parents, and we couldn't take the chance of retaliation. It kept us all safe, giving me enough time to explain. A nurse will take a swab inside your mouth for a DNA test, as well as mine. Do you consent?" I nod. "Meanwhile, Lana will get you a drink." He smiles at Lana, and she disappears to fetch my drink.

My mouth is swabbed along with Alberto's. The samples are carefully packaged and taken to the lab.

Alberto sits in his chair, leaning forward toward me. His hands are together in the praying position. "Marco, I want you to know that I never stopped loving your mother. She was the best thing to ever come into my life. I was heartbroken when she wouldn't see me after we'd been intimate. I questioned my actions and wondered all these years what I had done to deserve her abandonment. The move to Italy was indirectly because of my loss of Mia."

"I guess we'll never know what really happened now that she's dead, and Gino too. I could ask my grandmother for you. Her memory is sketchy, but she might remember something important."

"What I'll never understand is how her death was ruled a suicide. I knew her very well. Mia was religious and steadfast in her beliefs, just like your grandmother. Suicide wasn't a choice she would have made. I'm positive the choice she made to have you at such a young age was due to that fact. The unknown reason for her death keeps me up pacing the floors on many a night."

"Nana is also convinced that it wasn't a suicide. I was too young to be included in the details. But I'll try and think about that time in detail, and maybe I'll remember something. I've pushed away those memories for so long that it might take me some meditative time. It was shortly after my little sister drow… um … I mean Julia drowned. Did you know about that?"

"Yes, I've kept a finger on the pulse of the happenings in Mia's life. At the time of Julia's death, I wanted to reach out to your mother with my condolences. It proved to be too difficult to do in person because of Gino, so I sent flowers and a note."

I run my fingers through my hair and sigh. "No one ever really knows the impact they have on other people's lives. It's a shame my mother never knew how much you really loved her. I just recently was able to tell the person in my life how much I feel for her, and it's the best thing I've ever done."

He stands, and so do I. We shake hands, and he moves in to hug me. "I'm so happy for you, son." He stands back and says, "Lana will be back in a minute. I'll see you later. Make yourself at home."

Fifty-Six

VINCENT

WE ARE MADE to be very comfortable in the spectacular room with a view. Amelia is accompanied in by one of the guards with the most threatening expression. She's still in the little pink dress she wore in the wedding today.

"Daddy! Mom! You're here. Where's Marco?" She hugs us both.

"We don't know sweetie. They just have us locked in here. Are you alright?"

"I'm fine. They even gave me cookies and coffee."

"This is so strange…"

"Hello everyone, time to talk business. My name is Alberto Ricci. This is my lawyer Santo Garini."

Both men sit across from us at the table. The guard backs up against the wall. Amelia squeezes my hand to let me know she sees the same resemblance I do to Marco. Ricci obviously keeps himself in shape and cares for his appearance. We're probably around the same age but he looks more like Marco's older brother sitting there if not for the grey peppered throughout his hair and slight wrinkles around the eyes.

"As you know Mr. Dragonetti there's an interest in your company that Don Fiori squashed when he bought his forty-nine percent of the business. There's a contract out on Don Fiori as we speak. The people who want him dead are the same ones that killed Gino Fiori."

"Would that happen to be you?" I sit up straighter.

"Quite the contrary, Vincent. May I call you Vincent?" I nod. "Don Fiori and my grandfather Don Ricci are very close friends, since elementary school. Originally, I brought all of you here to do him a favor, but just minutes ago it came to my attention that he may have orchestrated the ultimate betrayal twenty- two years ago. My plans have changed since that possibility has come to light."

"Are you going to let us in on your plans?" I ask.

"Since Gianmarco Fiori has a contract out on his life and the man is pushing eighty, I feel the need to secure those shares of stock in your company. I want you to sell me your shares."

I stand and pound my fist on the table. "Absolutely not! I've built my company from the ground up myself. I won't just sign it over to you."

"You can and you will." The body guard grabs Amelia and puts his gun to her head.

Lucia jumps up and knocks her chair over in the process. "No wait! She's carrying your grandchild!!" Amelia's eyes get as big as saucers and tears flow down her cheeks. Ricci makes the guard let her go. "Listen, let me explain. My daughter is engaged to your biological son."

Amelia whispers to me, "How did you know?" I'm hiding my shock because I didn't know that she's pregnant. Saying that she is was probably a 'hail Mary' play against Ricci for Lucia. I just wink and put it off till later.

Alberto leans back in his chair and scrubs his hand over his beard. *I know blood family is worth more to him than anything. My wife is clever.*

He stands and paces. "Marco is engaged to her?" He points to Amelia. "I was told she is like a sister, am I mistaken?" We nod. "She's pregnant with his child?"

I nod. "You know Marco is your son?"

"There's been no DNA results but the resemblance is uncanny. You and your family have been in on the betrayal? How long have you known?" He steps closer his eyebrows tight.

Mimi gets in between us and I pull her arm. She puts up her hands. "No, I assure you we didn't know who you were. I found a picture at Gino's funeral, Marco's mom at graduation with Gino and *you*. I was dumbfounded at how much it looked like Marco. We didn't know any details of who you were until you showed your face today."

"I believe you for some reason. Maybe it's the joy of finding my son and grandchild." He smiles then just as quickly darkens. "I need to discuss Don Fiori's betrayal with my father. He's in ill health so tomorrow morning I will speak to him. We have your rooms ready. Marco will explain the rest of the details. Get some rest."

"Wait, I want to see Marco now!" Mimi says.

Ricci gestures with his chin in the direction of the door. The beefy guard opens it and guides us all out. Marco is in the hallway waiting. Mimi jumps up and climbs his tall frame wrapping herself around him.

"Are you all OK?"

We all confirm it together, as we are led to the rooms. Marco fills us in on how Ricci is protecting us from the Bonino family. It's in our best interest to stay put.

Fifty-Seven

MARCO

THE SUNLIGHT SHINES through a crack in the drapes forcing my eyes to adjust to the brightness. Amelia is next to me her hair covering her face. When I gently wipe it away, she grins and sighs. Her tight little body snuggles into mine and there's nothing better. Skin so soft and supple glides under my fingertips, up and down and around her body.

"Mmmm, that feels so fantastic. Can we avoid the world and just stay here in our cocoon forever and ever?"

"I wish, little one. You were so tired last night I didn't want to ask what went down in the room while I wasn't there?"

Her eyes are still closed and she mumbles sleepily. "They put a gun to my head and dad stopped them... told them I'm pregnant... grandchild."

I sit up. "What! That bastard! I don't care if he's my father! I'll kill him with my bare hands!" Catapulting out of bed, I grab my pants.

She opens her eyes and blinks a few times. "I'm fine. Get back here. They were trying to get my father to do what they wanted." She reaches her hand out from under the covers and her tits are uncovered. I drop my pants and let her pull me back into the bed. *She's irresistible.*

"Well, that's the last time they use you as incentive. Mark my words!" I wrap her in my arms and she leans back on my chest. I kiss her on the head. "How come you told your dad before me? I've been waiting for the day."

She turns in my arms and kneels. "I didn't tell… *what* you knew?" She raises both arms and slaps her thighs. "How is it everyone knows before I even confirm it? Why didn't you say something to me?"

"It's dangerous to tell your woman she looks pregnant. All sorts of negative thoughts go through their head."

She grins and then her eyes narrow. "How did you know I might be pregnant?"

"Well, your nipples are darker." I trace my finger around one and then the other. She trembles. "You always eat breakfast and you've given that up recently and last night you were faking a little too much at being drunk, an actress you're not."

She slaps my chest. "Thanks a lot Mr. smartass. How do you know all these signs?"

"Well…" I clear my throat. "Caitlin had a pregnancy scare a few months before we broke up. I studied up on the signs because I didn't believe her. We never had sex without a condom. She wasn't the most honest person and I felt it was a trap."

Mimi's eyebrows hit her hairline. "Was she really pregnant?"

"Nope. It was one of her last-ditch efforts to trick me into marrying her. Pure fiction."

"Bitch!"

"Yeah, let's bury that subject into the depths of hell." I pull her into me and squeeze.

"Speaking of subjects, I'd like to bury. There's something I have to confess." She backs up a little and I can tell she's serious. "OK I'm just gonna come right out and tell you that I knew Gino wasn't your biological father. Since the funeral."

"How?" *Another surprise, they just keep on coming.*

"The pictures Vanessa had all over the table had one of Alberto with your Mom and Gino at graduation. I swear it looked like you traveled back in time. He had to be your father or your clone."

"Why didn't you say something?"

"At the time I brought it to my dad and he already knew from Don Fiori. It was a secret he was sworn to uphold. We had no clue who it was in the picture then. You and I had already said goodbye and I was in Arizona. Not something I would tell you over the phone." She shrugs. "I felt my father would be in danger if I said anything to you."

"You were probably right. If anything happened to your dad, I would never forgive myself. It's OK, I know now."

"So, the fact that I knew, buried?" She waves her hand in a cutting motion.

"Buried!" I mirror the hand motion. Then smile. "We're having a baby!" I hug her tight again.

"Would you be upset if I said I'm hoping the baby has your father's eyes? She scrunches her face together. "He's a handsome guy, how does it feel to know what you'll look like in what eighteen years?"

"I don't know whether to laugh or be insanely jealous that you have a crush on my father." I tackle her and position my body over hers.

She puts her index finger to her lips as if deep in thought. "I probably shouldn't' have mentioned that." I tickle her, she's laughing and gasping for air. I let her escape and catch her breath enough to speak. "OK, OK, I'm sorry. You're the only man I'm crushing on. I promise." I kiss her hard, lips and teeth mashing together. She moans.

"The hormones make me so horny." Mimi gets up on her knees and throws one leg over me. "Let me make good use of this incredible morning wood staring me in the face."

Her tits bounce as she pistons her hips over mine. The sight and feeling drives me wild. She feels like a velvet glove wrapped around me. Her hair is loose and I reach up to slide my fingers through it bringing her down lips to lips. After kissing awhile, she bites my bottom lip playfully before sitting tall again. Sexy nymph picks her hair up off the nape of her neck as her hips sway faster. They slowly move from her hair to her collarbone, to her breasts, then down to her thighs. She uses her fingers to stimulate her center. I almost lose my self-control but she comes first, so I flip us both over and pound out an explosive orgasm for her before I lose my shit right along with her. Her face is flush and glowing while her eyes sparkle up at me. I can't wait to make her mine forever and meet our little one.

Fifty-Eight

VINCENT

"How did you think up that plan so quickly when they put the gun on Mimi? I ask in the morning. I'm shaving in the bathroom mirror with a brand-new razor and other toiletries left for us to use. My wife is sitting on the bed.

"No plan she is pregnant."

"What?" I rush out of the bathroom with half a face of shaving cream. "I'll kill him. How could he let this happen? Is that why he proposed?"

She gets up and gently leads me back into the bathroom. My wife always has a calming effect on me. "Don't go crazy, Vince. He's loved her all his life. He told me before I made him chase her to Arizona."

"YOU made him chase her?" I see my surprised reflection looking back at her in the mirror.

She rubs my back, soothing me. "I pushed things along to end their suffering. God's plan just sped up a little. They'll be married before the baby comes."

"When did she tell you?"

"She didn't tell me. I know our daughter and the signs. She's really carrying our grandchild."

"Our first grandchild." I turn and put my arms around my wife.

She looks up at me. "Don't be angry, be happy and thankful that the father is our Marco."

"I guess you're right." I smooch her on the lips.

The table is set for kings at breakfast. The sun pours through the floor-to-ceiling windows. People crowded together on the strip below look like ants. We all sit quietly, waiting for the patriarch of the Ricci family to make an appearance. Lucia made a joke earlier in our room when she asked if she had to kiss his ring. This is all so dramatic compared to the way we've lived our lives up until now. If I had known what I was getting myself into, I never would have asked for that favor. I can't even reach Don Fiori for advice. He's gone into hiding. I guess that's a good thing because if he's still breathing, I'm not the Don. Yet. I only wish I knew more about the customs of the council and maybe a loophole to get me out of this obligation with my head attached to my body.

"Good morning everyone, I trust you all slept well." Alberto walks in with his two-thousand-dollar suit looking ready for anything. Meanwhile, I'm in the same clothes I jumped into last night to get over here as soon as we could. "Good morning." I sit up straighter, at least.

He walks to the other side of the room and opens a door. When he returns, he's behind a wheelchair that sits his father, Don Pietro Ricci. The old man lifts his hand to greet us and mumbles hello. He is dressed as well as his son including jewelry adorning his wrinkled hands. When I see them folded in his lap, the rings make me smile inside at my wife's joke. Alberto puts him at the head of the table, and a server pours him coffee. While he drinks it, his son starts the meeting. He first introduces me, Lucia, and Amelia. Then *his* son.

"Marco, even though we haven't gotten back the DNA tests yet, I'd like you to meet my father and your grandfather Don Pietro Ricci."

Marco gets up, shaking the old man's hand with a cordial greeting. "You are exactly like Alberto twenty years ago. You are his son for sure. It's a surprise but a joy to find out I have another grandson. I welcome you, son, to the Ricci family," Pietro gushes, pulling Marco into a hug.

"Another grandson?" Marco straightens to look at Alberto. "Do I have other siblings?"

"Wow, I'm sorry, I forgot to tell you about Ramiro. He's your half-brother. His nickname is RAM, for his expertise with computer technology. He's out of the country right now." Alberto sits and clears his throat.

Marco nods. "And his mother? Is she your wife?"

"His mother is not in the picture. She left when he was a baby." His mouth and jaw are tight as if he tasted spoiled food.

"I see. I'd like to get to know RAM when he gets back." Marco sits back down next to Amelia.

"Of course," Alberto replies.

Don Pietro sits up in his chair as well as he can and addresses Marco. "I'd like to see your name changed to Ricci before I die. You have Ricci blood in your veins as well as your children who will bear our name."

Marco blinks and looks at Mimi. "This has all been so sudden, sir. I haven't given a thought as to my last name legally being changed. I suppose your right, but I have a successful business that bears the Fiori name and will speak with my lawyer as to how to proceed."

Just then, the bodyguard hands Alberto an envelope. His eyes go wide, and he smiles.

"Here are the results. I called in a favor to rush the order." He rips it open, biting his bottom lip. "Just as we all suspected, Marco is my son." He goes to his father and hands him the envelope. "Papa, you have a great-grandchild on the way too. Amelia is pregnant with Marco's child." He pats his father on the back.

"Dio Mio, we've been so blessed. Alberto, we should celebrate." The Don smiles at all of us with new vigor.

"We will Papa, we will." Alberto goes to Marco and hands him the results. Marco and Amelia look at it together. Alberto stands with open arms, and Marco gets up to hug his father.

The feelings coming over me aren't logical ones. I have an obligation to Marco as if he is my own son. God knows I've thought of him that way since he was little. It feels like they're taking him away from us. Consuming him. I guess I never had to deal with territorial feelings before because Gino was so distant from him. This is stupid. He's a grown man, for God's sake. His character is already ingrained, and he won't be changed by these people. He's marrying my daughter, so they will all be with us as a family. That feels better.

Alberto brings me out of my rumination.

"Your liaison with Don Fiori has been the reason we're protecting all of you here from the Boninos'. But in light of Don Fiori keeping my son from me all these years..."

The old man interrupts his son. "Alberto, you don't know for sure if Gianmarco knew his grandson was yours." He pounds a fist on the table.

"Papa, if this young woman figured it out by looking at a picture of me when I was young and comparing it to Marco, anyone can see it." He smooths his tie and pulls his cuffs.

Pietro lowers his chin, pushing it back. "Even though he and I have been friends, we never mixed with the wives and kids." He holds his wrinkled hands up, palms facing outward. "He never saw you after high school. We need to give him the benefit of the doubt. I will talk to him myself after the Boninos' are dealt with." That last word seems like gospel, and we all accept it.

Fifty-Nine

MARCO

We stay in Vegas an extra three days while my 'new dad' and his men take care of Carmine Bonino and his gang. I guess this stuff happens all the time in *the business*. Everyone wants the top spot. To be the BOSS. Except me. I want nothing to do with any of it. Vincent tells me that Don Fiori has known all along I wasn't his blood. From the time he found out, he swore I would not hold the top spot because I was the blood of a rival. Vince is still worried about what will go down between Pietro and Gianmarco if the Ricci's find out.

The threat to us is gone because the two top families are now blood-related to Amelia and me. Even though the Fiori family only has two members left, Vanessa and him. Don Fiori is the only person standing between Vincent becoming the head of the five families. Vince is in his office trying to come up with ideas to make everyone happy. I'm not sure that's possible.

At the doctor's this morning, we officially confirmed Mimi's pregnancy. As soon as Tony and Liz return from Hawaii, we'll get married. Planning our wedding has taken over the Dragonetti dining room table. We decided to have it at the house in Lake Geneva since Mimi wants to get fitted for her dress before a baby bump shows up. We've done away with having to worry about openings at a banquet hall. There are bridal magazines strewn all over the table, and Mama D and Meems are pouring over them. They hold up color swatches and then change their minds a hundred times. Pictures of cakes, dresses, and flowers are pinned up on a board. The pinning, my job for the last hour.

I clear my throat. "Meems, I think I'll go over and bring Vanessa some dinner." I can't wait to get out of here and leave the rest of the planning to the women. Except for the food and cake tasting, I am all in on that.

"OK, babe, mom made her a doggy bag, it's in the frig." She stands and kisses me goodbye.

The condo we just finished remodeling in my building has three bidders and should close by the end of the month. Everything is all locked up there as I pass by on my way home to check on Vanessa.

Music is pounding from her speaker, and she's got textbooks strewn all over the table. Van is taking classes all year round to finish early. She's interested in a hospitality and hotel management degree. When Vanessa graduates, I plan to ask Vincent to give her an internship. Even though her inheritance from her parents gave her more money than she could ever spend, she still needs a job to feel self-worth. Vanessa is as intelligent as she is beautiful. She has light brown hair with blonder tips and her mother's hazel eyes. Poor Marcella was too young and beautiful to die. Too bad she was in the car with Gino at the time the Boninos' executed the hit.

"Hey Van, have you eaten? I brought home chicken cacciatore from Mama D."

"Yum, let me at it." She dives for the drawer to get a fork and opens the plastic container. "Mmmm smells amazing." She shoves an enormous bite into her mouth and moans.

"Yeah, Mama D is the best cook I've ever known. She's been like a mother to me my whole life." I sit down at the corner from her.

"Do you remember your mom?" She tilts her head.

"Yeah. I was eight when she died, but I remember a little." A hollowness consumes my chest.

"I can still hear my mom calling my name sometimes." She has a vacant stare. "Is that weird?"

"Nah, I think it's great. Hold on to that." I move some books out of my way and lean in on the table. "There's something I have to tell you, Van."

"Yeah, what?" Her eyebrows furrow and then release.

"While I was away in Vegas, I found out that Gino wasn't my biological father."

"Seriously? Her head stiffly draws backward. "That means we're not…" I grab her free hand and squeeze.

"Blood-related." I sigh.

"So, you want me to move out?" Letting go of the fork, she gets up, putting her back to me. "I'm all alone."

"You're NOT alone!" I grab her and turn her to look at me. "This means nothing as far as our relationship. I learned from the Dragonettis' blood ties is not necessary to be a family and love each other like one. We might not have been close while Gino was alive, but we are now. We're family, Van. Nothing is gonna come between us, OK?"

She nods with teary eyes and hugs me around the waist. I'm happy that I could convince her she'll be taken care of, and I will always have her back. After all, it's not her fault who her father was and why her parents were killed. She needs me, and Amelia.

Sixty

VINCENT

MY BRAIN HURTS from going over many different scenarios to appease everyone in the council. Ricci wants to get back at Fiori by taking my shares, but I won't let that happen. The only Ricci I trust as the major shareholder in the company is Marco. The plan is to see if Alberto will accept Marco as the recipient of my shares. The Ricci-owned half of the company will be his. Then the forty-nine percent Don Fiori owns reverts back to me automatically as soon as I take over the top boss position in the family. Consequently, the company remains in the family through Amelia and me. There's one problem. Don Fiori.

Do I betray him by telling Alberto Ricci that he knew all along about Marco's parentage? It seems too much like I'd be playing with fire, no strike that, dynamite. Maybe, I can bargain with Fiori to step down and still be involved on the down-low. Offer him something he really wants.

There's also the fact that I really don't want the job either. I just might have to put my own wants aside in favor of keeping my legacy in the company safe. For now, I'll offer Alberto Ricci my shares in Marco's name then wait to see what happens with his relationship with Fiori. Marco should know first.

"Hey, did you come up with any ideas? "Marco asks as soon as he answers.

"I'm giving *you* my shares."

"Wait, what?" He clears his throat.

"The only Ricci I trust with my company is you. Alberto will have to be happy with you holding fifty-one percent of Dragon. But, I want to make sure that you're on board if he insists you change your name immediately. Are you comfortable with it?"

"Yeah, sure. Anything to make this easier for you. You'll still be CEO, right?"

"Yes, and if Fiori grumbles, I'll offer to buy back his forty-nine now instead of waiting to take over. And I'll remind him that he told me he had previous knowledge of your paternity." I shift in my chair and rearrange papers.

"Please only threaten him with that if you absolutely have to. He's not a man to try to push into a corner."

"We may not hear anything from him. He's still in hiding, not returning any calls."

"I'll get on it right away. Vince, I'm sorry you're involved in all this. Is there anything else I can do?"

"My bed was made when I asked Fiori to intervene for the company. It has nothing to do with you. Just make sure my little girl and grandchild are safe and healthy."

"They're my top priority."

Sixty-One

AMELIA

CLYDE LOVES to lie in the warm spots of sunlight on the floor. That's where I find him next to my bed on my wedding day. My summer childhood bedroom is so familiar, surrounding me with memories and favorite colors. My mom and I changed my room in the city several times during different stages. But this room at the house in Lake Geneva stayed relatively the same. I've been up for hours thinking about today.

My hand rests on my stomach, where a little person made up of Marco and me grows. I know it's crazy, but talking to 'Bud' makes me calmer. The flower analogy isn't lost on the fact that I've always admired how things of such beauty come to be. God exists in the fact that babies and flowers and everything else is born. And it all has such beauty.

"Well, Bud, today's the day I get to marry your daddy. He told me that he knew we were always destined to be together from the first time he saw me. I was only a little older than you." I pat my tummy and chuckle. "Maybe it's chemistry or a smell like pheromones? Or, what if we've been together in past lives and are destined to always meet again? It's what we call a mystery. When I saw your dad after coming home from college, that's when the pheromones kicked in for me. You see, I always loved him while I was a kid but now, I'm in love. I can't stop wanting to be with him. His perfect smile, twinkling eyes, and a body as strong and tall as a tree. Wait until he holds you way up there. You're gonna love it."

There's a knock at the door. "Come in." I sit up in bed and prop the pillow behind me. Clyde pops up and greets my visitor. She picks him up and scratches him behind his ears.

"Hey, kiddo, did you get any sleep at all? Are you talking to yourself?" Liz sits on my bed next to me, looking gorgeous, fresh from her honeymoon. "I know how you feel, the excitement takes over, and sleep takes a back seat." Clyde licks her chin.

I giggle, sit up, crisscrossing my legs, and facing her. "I was talking to Bud. He or she is not much for conversation but a very good listener." She smiles when I rub my belly.

"I used to call Tess 'Sweet Pea,' and at the time, our talks got me through some dark days. In fact, until I met her in Rio, she was always Sweet Pea to me. Since I gave her up for adoption as soon as she was born, I didn't give her a real name. Richard named her Contessa."

"That had to be awful. I can't imagine."

She puts her hand up to interrupt. "Today is a joyous, wonderful day. Let's not talk about unpleasant memories. I regret telling the story because I'm happy now with my beautiful daughter walking down the aisle ahead of me, throwing rose petals. The dark days are over." She hugs Clyde to her chest and speaks to him. "Right? My furry little friend knows just how to keep the joy flowing."

Liz gazes across the room at my wedding gown hanging high on the closet door. The bodice has cut-out leaves fluttering off it that flow down to the middle of my thighs on the skirt. It looks like they just floated there randomly and stuck. My hair will be worn down with beaded leaves of the same size pinned into it.

Another knock on the door, and my mom joins us on the bed with Tess. Clyde picks Tess to jump on, now licking her whole face.

"She just finished her waffles. He must be licking the syrup," My mom says. Tess is giggling and teasing the pup while we all laugh at them.

"Nervous, sweetheart?" My mom asks.

I shrug, "I'll be nervous when it comes time to give birth. Today is cake."

"Thirty years ago, on my wedding day, I didn't realize how nervous I was. I didn't sleep the night before. Early in the morning, my friend and I went to use our last opportunity to get color in a tanning salon. At that time, you could stay as long as thirty minutes in the tanning bed. The warmth made me relax and finally fall asleep. In the end, I had a mean sunburn on my wedding day and had to call the doctor on our honeymoon. I swelled up and had to stay inside the room in Hawaii. Forbidden to go out into the sun, I watched your father from the balcony. Daddy would wave as he went down the slide into the swimming pool beneath our room." She chuckles.

"Oh, mom, that's awful. At least you can laugh now." I hug her.

"Yeah, the worst part was getting on my textured nylons and kneeling in church with them on. That was painful."

"We don't even wear nylons anymore," Liz says.

"Don't remind me of how old I am. It's bad enough I'm already a grandmother."

"My grandmother!" Tess says.

"That's right, sweetie, pretty soon you'll share your grandma with the baby," Liz says.

Tess puts her hand on my belly. "The baby that lives here. Right?"

We laugh. The girls are here together on my special day, and it feels great.

Sixty-Two

MARCO

"Marco Ricci," my reflection in the mirror says back to me. My entire life I've introduced myself as a Fiori, I was Gino's son, the Don's grandson, now my whole identity has changed at the age of twenty-nine. My family is still connected, my father a capo, my grandfather still a Don. Even my new father-in-law is being forced to commit. How does this happen when the last thing I want to be involved with is organized crime?

The fog that was over the lake early this morning has dissipated. When the door to the pool house opens, the sun shines brightly through the opening. Vanessa is there in the sun smiling back at me.

"Hey, can I come in?"

"Yeah, sure, what's up?"

She holds out a long box with a blue ribbon around it. "I cleaned out the safety deposit box that belonged to Gino and found this sealed box with your name on it. I thought it might be important to you."

I take the box and see my name in fancy script handwriting on the top. "Thanks."

"Aren't you going to open it? I'll leave you alone."

"No, stay." She nods and sits, smoothing her dress.

I sit too. Carefully, I untie the ribbon and break the seal on the box. Inside, a letter on stationery with a flourishing letter M at the top.

My Dearest Son,

This is my declaration of hopes and dreams for you. Although, I am not able to be with you in person, please know, that I am always in your beautiful big heart. There will never be a day that I won't be watching over you.

It is my hope that you are independent of your father and the family business. I want you to be successful in your own right. Use your intelligence and talents to become what you dream of and go to work each day looking forward to it.

May you grow up to be the man I envision who is honest, loyal, and loving. May you find someone someday that you cannot live without. Treat them with respect and fidelity. Always kiss them hello, goodbye, goodnight, and good morning. Just that little act will keep the intimacy alive in your marriage.

I'm sorry I can't be there for you during all the important days of your life. Please know that if I had my way, I would be. There's a price we sometimes have to pay for doing the right thing. I'm not ashamed of my decision, but the regrets sometimes consume me. I love you with all my heart. Remember I am with you forever until infinity.

All my love,

Mommy

Vanessa has been reading over my shoulder, and her arms go around my shoulders to hug me. I put down the letter and wipe my eyes. She picks up the box.

"Let's see what it is."

I open the box to find a chain with a small charm fashioned into the symbol for infinity.

Van unhooks the clasp and puts it around my neck. I smile at her and stick it inside my shirt. We head over to the church together, and they direct us to the groom's quarters.

"You almost ready?" Tony barges into the room with a bottle of scotch and two glasses in hand. "I figure a celebratory toast is needed for you landing such a great girl."

I turn from the mirror and smile big. "Your sister's the best. I'll celebrate forever."

"Yeah, yeah, don't come complaining when she gets into her whining fits." He pours two fingers worth in each glass.

"I'm the one who always distracted her out of those. Remember?" We clink glasses.

Vanessa giggles at our banter and excuses herself after kissing me on the cheek.

"To you and my sister having a great life together with my new niece or nephew. Cheers." He pours another for each of us. "If you ever hurt her, I'm gonna kick your ass." He salutes me and downs his.

"No worries, my friend." I pat him on the back. "My new purpose in life is making Amelia and our child happy."

"Hey, I met the new fam. Alberto's sitting out there looking like the spitting image of you in a few years. Even your grandfather looks pretty good for his age. The biological genes are gonna hold up for ya." Tony hands me my tux jacket.

"I still need to meet my half-brother. He's out of the country right now, according to Alberto." I straighten my tie in the mirror. "Not sure yet what the story is there."

"It'll all come out bro, it always does." He pats me on the shoulder.

Vincent, Dominic, and Daniel all pile into the room at once. This feels like my real family since I grew up doing sibling things with all my brothers. There's a lot of joking around and ball bustin' just like always whenever the ladies are absent.

Dominic raises a glass. "To Marco, the new reigning shareholder of Dragonetti Hotels and Entertainment. I filed all the paperwork and got the confirmation yesterday. Cheers!"

"Thank goodness we have this option, so I can keep it under our family control. Alberto conceded to the idea after I showed him your name was legally changed," Vincent says.

"Then when Don Fiori kicks it, dad will inherit the other forty-nine back too. It was already in the contract between them," Dominic says.

Daniel stands up, shaking his head. "I'm glad I went into medicine instead of the family business."

"I never wanted to be involved in it either. I can't even escape it when my whole fucking lineage changes." I shrug and drink the last sip in my glass.

"Language Marco," Vincent smirks at me. "We are on church grounds."

"Yes, my *son*. Men use foul language, but the holy ground is where we behave ourselves." A voice comes from the doorway, and I turn to see Alberto Ricci. "I wanted to see you before the nuptials to give you a gift from your grandfather and me, so you can wear it on this special occasion."

Sixty-Three

VINCENT

MY SONS and I let Ricci chime in on the little party we're having before the ceremony. Alberto walks in like he owns the place and has a fatherly reign over Marco. He gives him a Patek Philippe Nautilus with a Black Dial and an 18KT Rose Gold Bracelet. The watch retails for just under a hundred fifty thousand. He could have put a down payment on a house for them. *Marco's never been the material type. But if he won't accept it, they might be offended.*

"Wow, Alberto, this is too much," Marco argues.

"Nonsense, nothing is too much for my oldest son. I want to be a family, spend time together, spoil you and my grandchild," Alberto grandstands.

No mention of my daughter…

The room goes quiet for a second, and Tony saves us from any more awkwardness.

"How about a toast? Here Mr. Ricci, a glass for you. Cheers to Amelia and Marco and to family."

"Cheers!"

All of us file out to the church filled to capacity. I wait in the back to escort my little girl down the aisle. From the day she was born, she's been my most precious thoughts, my most venerated human on the planet. All I've ever wanted for her is to be loved and valued the way I know she deserves. Marco shows that in every look and action. So, today I'm a proud father excited for his daughter to start her new life with a man I practically raised myself. What more could I ask for?

I shake off my thoughts to the sight of an angel walking toward me in all lace and fluff. She would probably hate that I describe her wedding dress that way, but hey, I'm a dad.

"Hi, daddy." She has watery eyes when I close the gap between us and hug her tight. She's still so petite, and it makes her look too young to be getting married. Her genuine smile tells me she's as ready as ever.

"You look beautiful, sweetheart."

"Thank you, daddy. I love you."

"Love you too."

She takes my arm, and the music changes inside the church. Everyone is looking back at the bride on my arm. When we reach the altar, I shake hands and hug Marco before kissing her and handing my beautiful daughter to him.

As I turn and go to my seat, I can't help but notice a guest I never expected. Don Fiori and Don Pietro are both sitting front and center *together*.

Don Fiori nods to me, and I do the same in return before taking my seat next to Lucia. The ceremony is elegant, and I manage to keep the thoughts out of my head and at bay to enjoy it. But as soon as the bride and groom return down the aisle, my joy is suspended. Sam leans over to whisper that the two bosses want a meeting. But Don Fiori will see me first alone.

All the way back to the house for the reception, I wonder what it is I'll be forced to do this time. These two men have been friends since childhood. Hopefully, I'm not the one singled out.

Sixty-Four

AMELIA

HUGGING my dad before walking down the aisle set off a tsunami of emotion. Call it pregnancy hormones or whatever. But if I were to describe myself as one of those silly memes, I'm the one with her heart beating out of her chest and blooming flowers sprouting from it. I have the most profound love for everyone here. Row after row of smiling faces and loving eyes on me, here to wish us happiness.

Then the most important face. Marco. The way he's looking at me will be engrained into my memory forever. His eyes speak volumes of his feelings for me. The emotion is so tangible I can touch it, taste it, feel it, surrounding me like a warm blanket.

The meaning of life is here, inside of me.

On Marco's face.

And in our vows to each other.

Family is truly what life is about.

We will have our own little threesome nestled inside a huge extended one who all love each other unconditionally.

"I'm so lucky," I whisper when daddy puts my hand in Marco's, and we step up on the altar.

"I love you," Marco whispers back. "You're beautiful."

I look up at him through my lashes and smile before the priest begins his sermon. Then the part where we say our vows is heavenly. Marco wrote the most amazing ones I've ever heard.

"Meems, I've loved you since the day you were born. When your little hand grasped, onto mine our souls conjoined together." His voice cracks. "We've been there for each other through every stage of our lives. Even though you were too young to know it, during my darkest days, you brought joy back into my world." Marco's eyes fill as he continues, causing wet tears to run down my cheeks. "Today, our love has taken on a new direction as we become husband and wife. We will continue to spend our lives together. I vow to love you unconditionally, make you happy, and give you the respect and understanding you deserve. With this ring, I pledge my unending love and fidelity forever and ever." He slides the wedding band on my finger. The ceremony ends without a hitch, and we kiss as husband and wife for the first time. It's a more chaste kiss than I desire, can't wait to get my new hubby alone.

At the reception, the lake is sparkling under the setting sun. Marco and I take pictures with the bridal party when the light is just right. Cocktails and hors d'oeuvres are served. Dinner music is played by the band. Light conversation wafts by on a warm breeze.

Marco seems preoccupied for a minute, and I follow his gaze. He's watching my dad and Don Fiori go into the house together.

"Think I should go with your dad as moral support? I kind of feel responsible for what he's been having to deal with."

"I think he'll be okay. You need to just enjoy our day and put those matters out of your mind. Dad will be fine."

I succeed at convincing him to have a few appetizers before we have to stand in the long reception line.

Sixty-Five

VINCENT

THE MEETING with Don Fiori before dinner is nerve-wracking. Since the sun has just set, I turn the lights on in my office. He sits in the wing-back, and his bodyguard waits in the hall. Once I offer him a drink, and he declines, I sit.

"It's a nice way for you to unite your families, this wedding between Alberto's son and your daughter. Congratulations." Fiori leans forward in the chair and clasps his hands.

"It wasn't planned. They fell in love. But, thank you for coming. An honor to have you here." I pick up my pen, it's my habit to play with it across my fingers, but I just shake my head and place it further up on the desk.

"I wanted to thank you for keeping my secret. Ricci must never know that I knew about Marco's paternity. Please assure me it will continue to stay that way."

"You have my word. But, with respect, due to the similarities in the features of his son, he may already have come to that conclusion. "

When we discuss the deal with Marco getting my stock, Fiori's no fool. He knows it edges his family out of the loop. The deal he makes me agree to in return is unsettling, to say the least. It's antiquated, unfair, and ludicrous. Again, my hands are tied since he still holds all the power in the council. He is even higher up than Don Ricci, so I can't ask Alberto to let this request of Don Fiori be overruled. My solution is to make him think I'm on board for now. Work a way to change his mind later.

Dinner is served, and we all have a great time listening to the toasts. The bride and groom cut the cake. A sweet table full of Italian specialties and an ice cream sundae bar round it out. Amelia and Marco have their first dance, and then I step in for the father-daughter dance. Marco grabs Lucia, and she smiles so big at the gesture it looks like she could burst with pride.

"Daddy, thank you for everything. The whole day was just beautiful. It's my dream wedding." Mimi kisses my cheek.

"You're welcome, sweetheart. I'd give you the world if I could." I kiss the tip of her nose.

"Marco said we're supposed to meet in your office after the dance. Alberto has a surprise. Do you know any details?"

"No honey, just that there's a meeting. Didn't know you and Marco were to come too."

The music ends, and we walk off the floor. Sam is standing next to Lucia and Marco, giving me the signal to go into the house.

Instead of my office, we go to the library where there's more room for everyone. The bride and groom are seated comfortably on the sofa, and I sit on one of the wing-backs with Lucia perching on the arm with me.

"Thank you all for taking a moment out of this special day for me to make my apology." Alberto Ricci walks in with one of my employees behind him. The kid is never dressed in a suit, so he looks different. Older.

Amelia speaks first, "Alex, I'm so happy you could come. Welcome to the party. Let me take you outside and get you some food and a dri…"

Ricci interrupts Mimi with his hand up palm out. "That won't be necessary Amelia, please sit and be comfortable. Let me explain." He sighs deeply and continues. "I'd like to introduce you to my younger son Ramiro Ricci."

"RAM is what my friends call me," Alberto's son says.

Marco, Mimi, and I have our jaws on the floor because we know this guy as Alexander Greyson. He's my top programmer in the gaming division of the company. Tony's been singing his praises.

"I apologize for deceiving all of you about Ramiro's identity. He wanted to work at Dragon, and he insisted on getting the job by his own skills and not his name. So, we created the alias." Alberto puts his hands out to the side. "Can you forgive and forget so we can commence being a family?"

"Family is everything!" Don Pietro steps into the room behind RAM and puts his arm around him. "Say you're sorry too, boy."

I'm busy wondering why the Don has thrown away his wheelchair. When RAM finally speaks, "I apologize too. Especially to Amelia because she was my intro to Tony. I lied to her, and I'm sorry." He looks at Mimi.

"This is just such a shock cause you look like a totally different person," Amelia says.

"I know. I was gonna tell you at coffee, but we never went." He and Mimi go off to talk in the hallway.

I decide to take the reins and smooth everything over, "We accept. I can understand Alex– I mean, Ramiro wanting to get the job on his own merit."

"Thank you, Vincenzo, my grandson meant no harm. My son, however, spying is another story." Don Pietro looks at Alberto and shakes his head. "Sometimes he thinks he's in a movie or something."

Alberto chuckles and even seems embarrassed. "Thanks, dad." He walks over to me. "We never found anything that would be a problem with going into business together. That's why we're now a family business."

"We've always prided ourselves on the company our family created. And now that Marco has the majority of the shares, we take pride in the fact that he is still and always will be our family," I say.

Marco beams and Alberto sticks out his hand to shake mine. We shake on the promise of a family-run business. Marco's face changes as he zeros in on Alberto's ring. It's the symbol for infinity in diamonds on a gold, thick band.

Sixty-Six

MARCO

I CAN'T BELIEVE this guy is my half-brother. Alberto and I look like father and son. Except for his eyes, there's hardly a resemblance in RAM to either of us. He must favor his mother's side, whoever that is. The story will come out sooner or later, I guess. I think back to how pissed I was when he took those pictures of Mimi. Obviously, he wanted to get her clothes off.

"Is he really a photographer with an art show, or was that bull too?" I ask Alberto.

He has a scowl on his face but recovers quickly and nods. "Ramiro has had art galleries interested in showing his work. He did well with the photographs of Amelia. I take it you weren't thrilled with the idea?"

"No, I wasn't." I shake my head. "And It's not gonna happen again."

He makes intimate eye contact. "Amelia's your wife now. What you say is written in stone." Point made.

"Thanks, I appreciate the respect." I nod and back up a step.

"That's what family does!" He puts his hands out, palms up. "We respect each other. When you get to know RAM better, you will both be friends. Just like he and Amelia already are." He winks.

I just nod, but I'll probably never trust my own brother near my wife or any other loved one. He sparks uneasy feelings in my stomach every time I've seen him. Whether he's Alexander Greyson or Ramiro Ricci, I don't trust him. We'll have to decide if I even want him working at Dragon enterprises. Now that I own fifty-one percent, I can get him canned if I feel like it.

Vincent looks like he wants to wrap this up ASAP. I take the hint from his look.

"Amelia, it's time we get back to our guests, all of us. It's our wedding day, and we're not dancing little one." I take her hand and swirl her away from RAM. She giggles and gives him a little wave goodbye.

The party is in full swing, and my girl and I are dancing the night away. We take pictures intermittently with guests. While posing for a snapshot out of the corner of my eye, there's RAM hitting on Vanessa. The memory of Amelia wanting to introduce them comes back to me.

"Hey babe, did you introduce Vanessa to Ramiro?" I make sure my voice stays even.

"Yeah, they're around the same age, and I thought they could be friends." She smiles.

"Looks like he's thinking more than friends. He's got his arm around her." I'm seething now that he's putting the moves on my ex-half-sister. The jerk is really coming on strong. I make a note to talk to Vanessa about him.

"Oh stop, he's just a friendly guy. Don't worry. Vanessa is smart and can take care of herself." Her hand is tapping on my chest.

I clear my throat. "I just don't want to walk into her bedroom and find photographs of her almost nude too." I kick myself as soon as the words leave my lips.

"Are you really bringing that up now on our wedding night?" She stops dancing and gives me her usual look when she's not happy with me. I don't even have to turn my head to know she's giving me *the look*.

"Yeah, sorry. You're right." I look away from the couple and zero in on my bride.

"Just always remember those two words, and we'll have the happiest marriage ever." She winks.

"Ha…ha." I chuckle and twirl her back onto the dance floor. Her smile is as big as I've ever seen it. She loves getting one over on me.

And I love her.

Sixty-Seven

MIMI

THE LIGHTS from the party reflect off the lake in lustrous swirls. While the soft breeze blows tendrils of my hair off my face. It's a perfect night for a wedding reception. Marco is on the floor with his grandmother in a wheelchair, dancing with her. I motion to the photographer to get a shot of it.

On her wedding day, a bride should get everything she wants. So, I insist on dancing with every one of my brothers. Tony's first. My brother Tony is the most serious of my three brothers. He's a workaholic. After Liz and Tess, he puts the company as a priority in his life.

"Kinda crazy that we didn't catch RAM was under an alias in the background check," Tony says.

"I think that Alberto Ricci can do anything he wants, including creating a believable alias for his son. Are you going to be able to look past the lies and still treat RAM the same as before?"

He twirls me outward and brings me back in before he answers, "There's no question the kids a genius when it comes to gaming. I'd be a fool to let him go because he's been a supreme asset. But I will keep a closer eye."

"I get it. When I saw him in the house, he looks like a completely different person than when we met." I bite my bottom lip. "He was dressed like a man and not a teenager. He had me fooled all this time that he was a military orphan. I actually felt sorry for him."

"It takes a certain type of person to lie like that for whatever the reason."

"I agree, but this is Marco's chance at a relationship with his real father. I don't want to take that chance away from him. Please keep an eye, but this is between you and me for now."

"Can I cut in?" Dominic steals me away from Tony. I reach up and hug my oldest brother, and he plants a kiss on my cheek before Dom and I dance. "Mom told me your wishes of having a dance with each of us." He smiles down at me.

Dominic is almost the exact duplicate of Daniel. Many people can't tell them apart. When they were little, I would tattle on them for switching places in the school. My mother would get mad and dress them differently. They would change into each other's clothes in the boy's bathroom. When they were a little older, she even threatened to color one's hair while they slept. She never did, and they never believed her either. When they grew up and went to separate colleges, it all stopped. Except, for the times when they switched for girlfriends, which I found out later.

Now, their personalities are different. Dom is serious, sentimental, and trustworthy to a fault. Even if it means hurting himself to help the people he loves.

"You look, beautiful sis. I'm so happy for you and Marco. Mom and dad are too. I always knew he was in love with you."

"Thanks, I love him too." I wink. "How's the new job going? You like working at Dragon?"

"I love it. Dad has me traveling all over the world next year to each hotel. I love being an attorney, and traveling while I work, is a dream come true." The music changes to a waltz, and Dom leads me in the steps.

"Mom's gonna miss you. So am I. Will you promise to come home when the baby is born?"

The music crescendos. We float around the dance floor, my dress catching the air. It's so much fun that I giggle while he speaks over the music, "I promise, wouldn't miss that for the world. Daniel is waiting on the edge of the dance floor. Mom must have rounded him up too." He gestures to the right and leads us over to him. "Congratulations, I love you, Mimi." His emerald green eyes are watering as he kisses my cheek.

"Always so sentimental, Dominic." Daniel acts like he's wiping a tear. "She's not leaving for the war. When they get back from the honeymoon, you can see her just like you do now."

"Quit bustin' my balls bro. Our little sister is married and all grown up. She's happy, and I'm happy for her. Jerk." He punches Daniel in the shoulder, hard.

They both laugh, and I start dancing with Daniel. It's just like always with them bustin' each other. But there are no two brothers I know who are closer than these two.

Daniel is a fun-loving risk-taker with a few narcissistic tendencies. But he has a huge heart and will always put family first. He's never been a guy that any girl could hold down. There's a different girl on his arm every time I see him. The female population can't resist a handsome brain surgeon. Or as he refers to himself at home, the sexy neurosurgeon.

"Seriously, sis, I'm so happy for you. Marco will take the best care of you and the little one." He kisses my cheek, then hugs me close and leads me around the dance floor. Daniel is the big hugger. He displays his feelings for someone with touch.

"So, if it's a boy, you'll name him Daniel after his handsome uncle, right?

I pull back to look him in the eyes. "Hmm, not sure about a name yet, but I'll take that under advisement."

"Maybe you're cookin' a little brain surgeon in there just like me." He gestures to my belly with his eyes.

"Well, if he or she has your brains, I won't complain." I snort a laugh.

"Thanks, sis, nice to know someone appreciates my intellectual side. All the girls only want me for my body." He chuckles and wiggles his eyebrows.

"Yeah, yeah, my brother the gigolo. Someday, you'll wanna settle down when you meet the right girl." I cup his cheek with my palm.

"Can I dance with my *right* girl?" Marco steps up.

"Absolutely, bro. We were just sayin' how right you are for each other. Here's your gorgeous bride." Daniel twirls and then dips me backward theatrically. Everyone around us claps. He bows and presents Marco with my hand. After we pair up, Daniel watches from the sidelines when I'm facing his way, he winks and blows me a kiss.

Marco takes me in his arms and leads the way. "My grandma spotted Alberto and started crying. She insisted that she talk to him. I brought her over, and they've had their heads together ever since. Do you think she's filling his head with her conspiracy theory about my mom?"

"If she is, Alberto will maybe get some of the answers he's been looking for."

The rose petals are thrown, sparklers are lit, and form a tunnel over our departure. Guests wave goodbye as we embark on our new life together. Someone put a 'Just Married' sign on the back of the limo with tin cans trailing behind us. You can bet it was my dad, he loves to throw something retro into the mix. Our special day has been spectacular, and I can't wait to get back to the hotel with my sexy husband.

Sixty-Eight

MARCO

IT'S BEEN six months since our wedding, and Mimi has a round beach ball belly. The doctor says it could be any day now. We opted out of knowing the sex to be surprised on little one's birthday. I don't care, boy or girl is fine as long as they're healthy and Mimi is too.

Mama D has been making dinner for us to keep Meems off her feet. It's Sunday, we're all around the table when the door opens, and Dominic walks in.

"You're home!" Mama D runs to hug Dominic. "We've missed you, son."

"You kept your promise." Mimi hugs him too, but from the side to give the beach ballroom.

"Of course! My little niece or nephew is gonna know Uncle Dom." He reaches into his carry-on and produces a cuddly soft bear for the baby. "This bear is to remind you guys to talk about me to the baby while I'm traveling. And of course, I'll video chat with you too."

"I love you, Dom," Mimi says, hugging him around her belly this time.

"Uncle Dan will be around to keep the baby company while you're gone." Daniel steps up and teasingly shoulders Dominic out of the way to hug Mimi too.

"We'll be the babysitters!" Liz yells while Tess jumps up and down, clapping her cute little hands.

Tony just shakes his head, grinning. "It'll be good practice cause we're right behind you by eight months." Liz nods her head, confirming the good news.

Mama D jumps up from her chair. "Really! Oh my gosh, Vince, we're going to be knee-deep in grandchildren." She hugs Liz and Tony. "Christmas is going to be so much fun."

Everyone congratulates Liz and Tony with hugs and a champagne toast. Fruit juice for the mommies' to be and Tess.

In bed, while the moonlight filters through the blinds. Mimi is in my arms resting, my fingers lightly draw lines on her skin. My mind, as usual, is in the gutter.

"Hey, I read that sex escalates the birth. You wanna try and hurry up this baby?"

She looks up at me rolling her eyes. "I don't feel very sexy impersonating a beach ball about to pop."

"What happened to the hormones making you horny?"

She sits straight up, holding her stomach, and growls.

"Ok, I get the picture… Wait…What's happening? Is it time?" I rub her back as the pain subsides.

"I think it's Braxton Hicks again. Will you do your magic to relax me, baby?"

The last time, Meems had these false contractions, we called the doctor. He assured us in the office that it wasn't time yet. She told Mimi to masturbate or have me help her have an orgasm to help with the pain. I'm always happy to oblige, cause my girl is making a human in there. There's no greater love I've ever felt than this sacrifice she's making for our future.

"Just relax. I'll take it from here."

Another pain ramps up, and her growl is louder this time. I open her legs and massage her, making her growl turn into moans. She finally falls back to sleep after her orgasm. I slip out of bed and go into the bathroom to calm my erection. I sit on the edge of the tub. Run my fingers through my hair, and study the tiles beneath my feet.

"Hey, I have to go to the bathroom." Mimi walks toward me and sits on the toilet. "Umm, this is weird. I'm peeing, but it doesn't feel like it. I can't stop and start it like usual."

"Could it be your water broke?"

"I don't know. I always thought it would be a big gush. This is a steady trickle."

"It must be leaking." I grab my phone and call the doc. "They'll call back in a minute."

When the phone rings, it's the doc telling us she'll meet us at the hospital. Mimi must put on baggy sweat pants with a towel between her legs for transport to the maternity ward. The doc comes in to check her and says it won't be long.

The next morning, after five hours of labor, our daughter Mia Lucia Ricci is born. Mama D insists we not use her name as our daughter's first name even though that was our intention all along. She loves my mother's name, Mia.

Two days later, we're home at the condo, and Vanessa is holding the baby, finally distracted from staring at Daniel. The whole place is filled with gifts, balloons, and family. Everyone couldn't wait to meet our princess. It's amazing how babies bring everyone together. We have Alberto, Pietro, and RAM representing the Ricci's. Gianmarco and Vanessa are Fiori. And all the Dragonetti's. Vincent, Lucia, Tony, Liz, Tess, Daniel, and Dominic.

Mama D cooked a meal for kings, and we all sit down and eat together. I can tell Vincent is still on edge about the fact that he's still stuck between loyalty to Don Fiori and Don Ricci. I convince him to put that aside for now and enjoy his granddaughter. Vince has Mia in a football hold on her tummy with her pacifier in her mouth. She's quiet and comfy while he sings to her in a whisper.

The dishes are done, and everyone leaves us alone with our princess. She's sleeping soundly in her bassinet. Amelia and I are on the sofa, her head in my lap. I stroke her silky hair, and she moans, "I wish we didn't have to wait so long to have sex."

"It's for you to heal. Don't worry, little one, I'll go back to blowing your mind with the *Fiori fantasy* before you know it." I kiss her forehead.

She giggles. "I think we better rename it. I'm just perfect with the *Ricci reality* from now on. I love you."

Epilogue

AMELIA

The first year of Mia's life was spent in bliss. Marco and I were happy to be able to stay home with our daughter due to a pandemic. We filled our days with projects, cooking, baking, and sex. Fall started out with a bang finding out I was pregnant again. The babies were eighteen months apart. A healthy eight-pound baby boy we named Marco Anthony Ricci graced our family. Two in diapers at the same time was daunting, especially after Marco went back to work. But we got through it together. My mom is always around to help, thank goodness.

Tomorrow's Mia's third birthday, and we're celebrating at my mom and dad's house. I'm in the kitchen making meatballs and staring into the den from the kitchen island. My husband has our daughter at the same little picnic table we played with together when I was three, and he was ten. My mother keeps everything. It's set up with all her dolls and stuffed toys. Marco doesn't fit on the seat, so he sits on the floor next to her, pretending to drink tea from her play tea set. I didn't think my heart could grow any bigger. But the sight makes it feel like it could burst.

"I remember when he was ten, and you were almost four. He would play like that with you for the whole time Anthony had his music lesson," Mom says, wiping her hands on a dishtowel.

"I picked a great one, mom." I put my arm around her shoulders.
"You sure did, sweetheart." She kisses my cheek.

***Vanessa is in love with Dominic's twin brother. It was really him she
slept with. Telling her they switched could mean the end of her trust
in him and a life-long prison sentence.***
Claim your copy of the next book in
The Connected Series.
Consigliere

CONSIGLIERE

Thank you so much for reading *The Deleted Heir*; please consider
leaving a REVIEW. Please share the link with me at Theresa@
theresapapa.com. I would love to read it!

REVIEWS

Reviews are crucial in helping other readers choose their next book and you can help them by leaving a few sentences about this book as a review. If you don't have time or feel confident writing one, recommending a book to your friends, family, and coworkers can help them in the search for their new favorite read. Thank you again for your support!

Meet Eve and Ian in Theresa Papa's next series. The *Fall from Grace Series* begins with <u>Prodigal Billionaire</u>, a grumpy single-dad romance.

A devastating betrayal.
A man driven into seclusion.
A woman with a devoted heart.
Perplexities of their private lives threaten their reputations.
Can love thrive in the face of truth?

PRODIGAL BILLIONAIRE

Want to know details on freebies and all the upcoming new novels from Theresa?

NEWSLETTER

**Love The Deleted Heir? Go back to the beginning where it all
started in the prequel.
The Misconception of Mia.
FREE for a limited time
Click HERE.**

FREE BOOK!

About the Author

Theresa is blessed to be married to her main man for thirty-five years. She knows what it takes to have a loving, lasting relationship. Her husband keeps her laughing after all this time. Tips on keeping the sparks alive along with the witty banter appear in her writing regularly. Her tagline "Add some spice to your life, read Romance" is a clever way of describing the feelings her writing evokes.

Love stories, a little suspense, and the happily ever after are Theresa's prescription to keep you smiling. She is ecstatic to share her characters with the world and entertain her readers. Her big Italian family extends throughout the country with a rich and flavorful history. Much of that history spurs ideas for the stories she creates. Make sure you visit the _Art Imitates Life_ in the back of every one of her books. It's fun to see where ideas are born.

If you enjoyed reading _this book_. See more of all the characters in Theresa's fictional world. Use the QR code below.

WEBSITE

"Art Imitates Life"

A NOTE FROM THE AUTHOR

'Art imitates life' is true about certain details in the story of Amelia and Marco. It might be interesting for you to know some of the elements that are somewhat born out of reality.

- The scene where Amelia tells Marco that her classmate grabbed her boob and she kicked him comes from my own reality in fifth grade. The boy and I were suspended for three days.
- The scene where Samantha says she had to lie down in the car to fit with the Bride of Frankenstein hair also comes from my own reality. My hair was two feet high with the white lightning bolts and all.
- The scene where Marco saves Tess from drowning really happened to my husband in Lake Geneva at the pool. He dove in to save a little boy from drowning. Tony was fully dressed, wristwatch and shoes included. After he put the little boy in his mother's lap the mom never even said thank you. She just yelled at the little boy.
- Lucia never charges her phone, that's me. My kids have to call my husband's phone if they want us.

- The story Lucia tells the girls about getting sunburn on her wedding day? Guilty! I had such a difficult time getting dressed. And spent the first three days in Hawaii in the hotel room swollen.
- The scene where Amelia's water breaks is exactly what happened to me with my first child.